HERO IN CAMERA

The Justice Thalia Stories
Snowfall
Murder Most Fowl
The Sweetest Poison

888-555-HERO
Hero De Facto
Hero Ad Hoc
Hero De Novo
A Very Hero Christmas
Hero De Jure
Hero In Camera
Hero Amicus Curiae
A Very Hero Wedding
Hero Ad Litem

Solar Systems Services, Inc.
Alone is Not Lonely

Millersburg Magick Mysteries
Spells and Sleuths
Fae and Felonies
Magick and Murder

Soccer Moms of the Apocalypse
Pestilence in Pumpkin Spice (Coming Soon)
Famine In French Vanilla
War in White Chocolate
Death in Double Mocha

Miscellaneous
Sword and Sorceress 31 ("Pig-Headed")
Sword and Sorceress 32 ("Unexpected")
Practical Witches
Revenge Served Hot
The Yule Switch

For updates, news, and giveaways, join Suzan's mailing list or visit her website at www.suzanharden.com. You can also check her out on Twitter or Facebook.

This is a work of fiction. All characters, organizations and events in this novel are products of the author's imagination and are not to be construed as real. Any resemblance to persons, living or dead, is entirely coincidental.

HERO IN CAMERA (888-555-HERO #6)
Copyright 2020 by Suzan Harden
All rights reserved
ISBN: 978-1-64918-007-0

Published by Angry Sheep Publishing
Findlay, Ohio

Interior Design by JW Manus
Cover Design by For the Muse Designs

Hero in Camera

888-555-HERO #6

Suzan Harden

PROLOGUE

Tim Canyon, the retired superhero/vigilante known as Jatz'om Kuh, the Ghost Owl, got up from the arm of the ugly turquoise couch where he perched. He didn't have the heart to tell Harri how much he hated the color. And doing so while his live-in girlfriend was obviously distressed would likely blow their relationship to kingdom come. The ring box in his jeans pocket shifted, but now was definitely not the time. So much for his dinner plans tonight with her.

He set the damning photographs in his hand on top of the banker box next to Harri and held his hands out for her. She let him pull her up from the huge rug that covered most of the floor of their loft living room. A gold and turquoise rug that matched the godawful couch. He wrapped his arms around her slight figure.

"Right now, all we have are pictures," he murmured into her apple-scented hair. "This was when Trubble was a young officer. Back when he and Eagle Forever were still on speaking terms. Well before you were born."

"What if this is what caused their rift?" Harri leaned back and gestured at the pictures. "What if Grandma Harri and Trubble were helping Lydia get away from her own father? What if—"

Tim laid his right index finger over Harri's lips. "We can 'what if' until the cows come home, honey. Why don't we take the boxes down to the basement for now? I can do some cross-checking and see if I can find out what happened."

"What if Lydia's baby was the first super infant Trubble stole?" Harri stared up at him with watery eyes. It wasn't like her to cry over, well, anything. But when it came to children, she had a huge soft spot.

Especially for someone who claimed she hated rugrats.

"That's the problem, honey." Tim leaned his forehead against hers. "We have no idea what happened. Have you gone through all the boxes yet?"

"No," she admitted.

"Why don't we go out and get some dinner first? Then I'll help you to organize the rest of the contents?" he suggested.

"I really don't feel like going out," she murmured.

"How about I pick up an order from Marta's and I'll help you go through the boxes?"

"O-okay," she said.

"Harri, for as rude and condescending as your grandmother could be, she wouldn't deliberately harm a child."

She laughed, sniffed, and wiped her eyes at the same time. "Didn't you tell me she threatened you when you were twelve?"

"She didn't follow through with it." He chuckled. "And I bought an awesome robotics kit with the bribe she gave me."

"Was that kit worth seeing my grandmother and your grandfather having adult time on his office desk?" Harri grinned.

"What are you talking about? I had forty bucks that said I saw nothing of the kind." Tim grinned back and pulled Harri close to him. He just prayed he could divert her from whatever they found in those damn boxes. The last thing he wanted was to see all of Harri's perceptions of her beloved grandmother ruined by the truth.

CHAPTER 1

❖

One month later . . .

Harri Winters smiled across her office desk at Mother Defiant, who sat on one of Harri's visitor chairs. The superhero's white coif, veil and wimple were at odds with her skintight black unitard and shiny black boots. Everything happened exactly as Winters and Franklin's newest partner Susan Kennedy had predicted a little over a year ago.

"I don't understand why I can't simply talk to Susan," Mother Defiant said haughtily.

"Because I'm the senior partner." Harri kept the smile plastered on her mug though she really wanted to leap over her desk and smack the attitude from the superhero's pretty face. "I do the intake interviews, but the entire partnership has a vote on whether to accept a new client."

"But I'm not a new client!" Mother Defiant protested.

"You are to this firm." Harri shrugged. "And frankly, we'll be taking a very long and very serious look at you. Especially after the way you dumped Susan for Dewey and Cheatham."

Mother Defiant's cheeks flushed bright pink. At least, she had the grace to be embarrassed. When she could finally meet Harri's eyes again, she said, "I should have known they were only using me. The reason I want to speak with Susan is I owe her a very big apology."

At the knock on Harri's office door, she yelled, "Come in."

Tim Canyon sauntered in with Mother Defiant's cell phone in his hand. "I've cleaned off the spyware and added extra protection. No one will be tracking you anymore."

"Tracking me?" Mother Defiant looked appalled.

"Was it the source of Susan's infection last year?" Harri asked.

"Definitely." Tim held out the phone to Mother Defiant. "You're clean now, but you might want to inform any superheroes you've come in contact with over the last year. I'll clean up their devices free of charge."

"What?" Mother Defiant looked wildly at Harri and Tim, totally flabbergasted. "Who?"

"Corvus used spyware on your phone to get a bug into our office last year," Harri said.

"But I wasn't a part of that crap!" Mother Defiant protested. "Not to mention they're all in jail now." Her eyes widened as she put two and two together. "Dewey and Cheatham were part of Corvus?"

"We don't know anything for sure at this point," Harri said as evenly as she could. While the Winters and Franklin staff suspected a link between the rival law firm and the out-of-control black ops group, the last thing Harri needed was a slander lawsuit against her fledgling business.

"If you need anything else, buzz me." Tim winked at Harri before he sauntered out of her office, closing the door behind him.

"I still can't believe your head of security is Tim Canyon."

Harri smirked at the superhero's comment. "He was acquitted during his murder trial, and the Ghost Owl exposing Corvus proved Seismic Shift killed Tim's wife and son, not him."

Mother Defiant sagged in her chair. "Is that why I can't talk to Susan directly? She thinks I set her up? That I was part of the Corvus conspiracy?"

Damn. Harri hated even thinking about those assholes. But she would be naïve to believe the FBI sweep captured all of Corvus's allies. While she wanted to give Mother Defiant the benefit of the doubt, Harri couldn't risk the lives of everyone she loved.

"As I said, the entire partnership will discuss whether or not to take you on as a client," Harri said firmly. "My question is why do you want a firm outside of Hermanville."

Mother Defiant took a deep breath. "I've been dating Blue Racer. Dewy and Cheatham were charging me for every little thing. I barely have enough from my licensing contracts to live on, and I'm tired of ramen noodles every night for supper. Blue said he was super happy with what your firm did for him, and when I found out my old attorney worked here, I decided to change representation."

Harri tapped the copy of the dismissal letter Mother Defiant provided. The superhero was smart enough to provide copies of the certified mail and return receipts, showing the letter was delivered and signed for at Dewey and Cheatham. They left Harri in the clear to talk to Mother Defiant because Harri had no doubt Howard Dewey would file a complaint with the bar regardless of whether she and the superhero had danced the right steps.

"All right." Harri nodded. "I'll start calling your references this afternoon. Assuming everyone gets back to me right away, you should hear from me in two days."

"Thank you for considering me as a client." Mother Defiant's smile was weak. She obviously figured this was a lost cause, but Harri still planned to follow through on checking reference and discussing representation of the superhero with her partners. Even if she did want to inflict a little payback for how Mother Defiant treated her firm's newest partner and her friend.

They both rose from their chairs, and Harri escorted Mother Defiant to the front doors.

After the final good-bye with the superhero and her departure, Harri walked back into the reception area, the original foyer of the Lechuza Building. She was still impressed how good their building manager Miguel Esperanza made the original Art Deco design look when his team renovated the place.

As she passed the reception desk, their assistant Patty Ames winced and put a call on hold. "Harri, your ex-husband is on line 1."

Now, why the hell was Eddie calling her? The new Mrs. Lewis had thrown a major hissy fit about him talking to Harri. It didn't matter that things were long over between them, or how much Eddie adored Sarah and their two kids. She was one insecure woman. Therefore, if Eddie was calling, it was business-related.

"Thanks, Patty."

Harri strode into her office and sat down to compose herself before she picked up the receiver on her phone set and jabbed the button next to the blinking light. "Hey, Eddie! Does Sarah know you're off the leash?"

So much for any composure.

"Not funny, Harri," he snapped. "This is business." Of course, it was.

"And what can I do for Canyon Pointe's FBI office today?" she teased as she leaned back in her chair.

"Have you spoken to Miss Purrception lately?" Eddie said.

"Not since last month," Harri answered. "We're still fighting the extraditions to France and Brazil. Why?"

"Are you sure?" Eddie sounded more tense than usual.

"Eddie, out of all our marital problems, I've never out-and-out lied to you," Harri said. "Either spit out why you called, or hang up."

"Miss Purrception escaped from Mauvaises Prison last night."

"What!" Harri bolted upright.

"It gets better," Eddie added. "Byron Trubble escaped with her."

Harri's heart lodged in her throat. Retired General Byron S. Trubble. Former head of the secret black ops organization known as Corvus.

And the one person who wanted Harri dead more than any other supervillain in the world.

<h1 style="text-align:center">Chapter 2</h1>

———◆●◆———

Aisha scribbled notes on her legal pad concerning the contract proposal for Black Falcon's endorsement of a security system when there was a knock on her office door.

"Come in!"

The door opened, and Patty poked her head around the corner. "FBI red alert."

"Why the hell is Eddie calling her?" Aisha frowned. She handled matters between their clients and the Canyon Pointe FBI office because Sarah had some weird obsession Harri was trying to get Eddie back. Hah! Like that was going to happen when Harri had an ex-superhero warming her bed.

Arthur Drallhickey's head appeared above Patty's. "Because there was a mass breakout at Mauvaises Prison before dawn this morning, including Miss Purrception and Byron Trubble."

"What?" Aisha tried to wrap her head around their IT manager's words. She couldn't breathe. She and her husband Rey had gone to bat for the supervillain when she claimed she wanted to reform. Hell, they owed her after she helped them take down Professor Paranoia in Japan last year.

And pissed didn't even describe what Harri would be once she heard—

A screech of rage came from the direction of Harri's office. Patty and Arthur jumped into Aisha's office and closed the door.

"Has this reached any of the news outlets yet?" Aisha said.

Both Patty and Arthur shook their head.

"How did you—"

Aisha's office door opened again. Susan Kennedy, their third partner, and Miguel Esperanza, their maintenance man, slipped inside. Susan closed the door and locked it behind them.

"Please tell us Mother Defiant pissed her off," Susan begged. "Or Tim did something stupid."

Aisha shook her head. Besides, if Harri had a fight with her current boyfriend, they'd be on the fifth floor having loud, noisy makeup sex. Aisha had managed to snag a few boxes of the earplugs their client Nix endorsed for herself and Rey. She prayed little Mitch's powers didn't develop before she had to explain what Aunt Harri and Uncle Tim were doing.

It was bad enough Rey was probably listening to everyone's conversations from the fifth floor. Thank god, her brother-in-law Steve had taken his girlfriend and her son whitewater rafting with some of his friends visiting from Seattle.

At Harri's second shriek, Miguel stared at the ceiling. "*Madre de Dios.*"

Aisha sucked in a deep breath, eyed Patty and Arthur, and tried again. "How'd you two find out about the prison break?"

"When Eddie called and asked for Harri instead of you, I knew something was wrong," Patty said.

"Patty told me, so I took a quick peek in the FBI computers—" Arthur started.

Susan jammed her index fingers in her ears and started yelling, "La-la-la-la-la-la-la!"

"Cut it out!" Aisha snapped. "Your fingers aren't any cleaner than anyone else's at this firm. Or do I need to bring up your little gift to Harper?" Both Susan and Aisha had contributed money for a fresh start to Doctor Liquidation's former minion. The girl had a rough life before the supervillain rescued her from the streets.

Susan withdrew her fingers from her ears. "Harper may have been a minion, but she was never formally charged with any crime."

"But she did confess to the burglary at the San Francisco Federal Reserve." Aisha waved her hand. "How is that any different than what Arthur does?"

Susan held up her hands in surrender. "All right. Fine. You're right." She turned to Arthur. "I apologize."

"Thank you." Arthur inclined his head to her before he turned back to Aisha. "This gets worse. Black Death and Hard Knock escaped with them."

Aisha sat back in her chair. Her pencil shattered in her grip. This was why she had to give up ballpoint pens for every day work. Superstrength and anger resulted in two of her suits getting ruined by ink going everywhere.

"Any leads?" she asked coolly, trying to control her own temper.

Arthur shook his head. "That's why Eddie is calling Harri." He and Patty exchanged nervous glances. Cade Wilson hadn't been straight with Patty about his super status as Black Death. When he broke up with her, she hadn't told him she was pregnant. By the time Cade learned about his daughter Grace, Patty and Arthur were living together. Cade hadn't taken the news his ex was dating a former supervillain well, which was ironic considering he was Corvus's top wetworks agent.

"Patty! Aisha! Where the hell is everybody?"

From their winces, everyone in her office could hear Harri without the need of superhearing.

Aisha sighed. "Let's get this over with."

Susan was closest to the closed office door. She twisted the lock, opened the door, and yelled, "In here, Harri!"

The stomping got closer until Harri appeared in the doorway. Her gaze traveled from person to person, leaving Arthur quaking in his shoes, until it rested on Aisha.

"What the hell is going on in here?" she snapped.

"Our staff is hiding from you because they know how you get when you've been speaking with your ex-husband," Aisha bit back.

Harri closed her eyes and inhaled deeply before she released the air. "I'm not angry at Eddie. Miss Purrception escaped from Mauvaises Prison." A few heartbeats passed before she said, "Isn't somebody going to tell me I-told-you-so?"

"I told you so." Tim appeared in the doorway behind Harri. "What part of 'Please don't represent my former—'" His face turned red as he struggled to find a semi-polite term for the supervillain with whom he used to have casual sex.

"Feline fling?" Aisha offered.

"Boink buddy?" Patty suggested.

"Supervillain with benefits?" Susan chimed in.

"Party puta," Miguel declared with a disgusted tone.

"The furry skeleton in the closet." Harri crossed her arms and glared at Tim.

He looked at Arthur. "Don't you have an insult to fling?"

Arthur lifted his chin, which was nearly as pointy as his nose. "I may be a former supervillain myself, but I am not stupid enough to get in the middle of an argument between you and Harri."

"Arthur's right." Aisha leaned her elbows on her desk. "This bickering isn't helping the situation. Did Eddie give you any more information than she escaped with Trubble, Black Death, and Hard Knock?"

Harri shot her a nasty look. "Were you eavesdropping on my phone call?"

"I didn't have to," Aisha said calmly. "Arthur and Tim have search programs running for any information regarding known Corvus operatives in an effort to trace the remaining members. Arthur was already exiting his office to let us know about the escape when Patty transferred Eddie's call to you. It didn't take a genius to put two and two together."

"Oh." All the ire faded from Harri's expression to be replaced by guilt.

It almost made Aisha feel guilty about her little white lie regarding Arthur's timing.

Almost.

"God," Harri muttered. She wiped her palms down her face before she added, "I was so stupid to believe she really wanted to rebuild her relationship with her mother and daughters."

"You're not the only one she fooled," Aisha growled. "I thought she'd changed when she helped Rey, Steve, and me in Japan. I never would have agreed to represent her otherwise."

"I think you two might be jumping to conclusions." Susan stared thoughtfully at one of the prints on Aisha's walls.

"What makes you say that?" Harri demanded.

"Two reasons." Susan turned to face them. "First, turning herself in was the only way to get close to Trubble. She still blames him for losing custody of her daughters years ago, but she's not stupid enough to kill him on the prison grounds if what she's really after is revenge against him.

"Second, what if Black Death threatened her or Hard Knock? From her dossier in the National Superhero Bureau database, she and Knock are pretty tight. Every time she's escaped, she's taken him with her, but they part ways after the escape. She's only ever double-crossed people who've either screwed her over or planned to. Whatever their real relationship is, she does care about what happens to Knock."

"So, it's a question of which game she's really playing." Miguel scratched his beard.

"Miss Purrfection still broke her word to us," Aisha growled. "And I want her head on a platter."

CHAPTER 3

Aisha's declaration worried Harri more than a little bit. Even Miguel and Arthur glanced at her partner with concern on their faces.

Harri cleared her throat. "Why don't the rest of you get back to work? Aisha, Susan, and I need to discuss some partnership issues anyway."

Susan groaned. "Can I please get another cup of tea before we discuss your client intake meeting?"

"I need a mocha, too," Aisha added.

"Well, if you're all leaving Aisha's office to get drinks, we will have this meeting in my office," Harri said. "Where my coffee is still sitting on my handy-dandy coffee warmer."

They had a decent amount of revenue coming in on Tim's little device. The pre-orders for Christmas were already good when they'd advertised the coffee warmer in several business magazines as the latest must-have for busy executives. After a top-rated women's talk show claimed it was great for busy moms, too, the pre-orders shot through the roof.

Everyone walked out of Aisha's office. Tim glanced at Harri, but she ignored him, charged back to her own work space, and plopped in her chair. She took a sip of her own, still warm, coffee. She simply couldn't deal with him and his former fuck buddy.

So many emotions mingled in Harri she couldn't decide which one to focus on. Yeah, she was jealous of the supervillian because Miss Purrception was older than her and hot as hell. On the other hand, Miss Purrception had been screwed over by her baby daddy Captain Mojave and her daughters had been taken by Trubble, which was the reason she turned to villainy to begin with. But the thing that pissed Harri off most was all the work she put in negotiating Miss Purrception's reduced sentence and fighting the extradition attempts by other nations.

The cinnamon taste of her drink helped sooth her scattered feelings. Patty was right. A spoonful of the flavored syrup in black coffee made the morning a little brighter.

Susan strolled in with her steaming giant mug of tea. "Should we separate the Owls? They're in the break room discussing plans on how to capture Miss Purrception."

Harri rolled her eyes. "Trubble's the one that concerns me. What the hell was Miss Purrception thinking? He won't hesitate to kill her now that she's got him and Black Death out of Mauvaises."

"But why?" A crease appeared between Susan's eyebrows as she sat on one of the visitor chairs.

"Why what?" Harri asked.

"Why escape now?" Susan set her mug on Harri's desk. "Trubble and Black Death have been in prison for nearly a year. Trubble and Miss Purrception hate each other. What would make the two of them join forces? And why did they escape now?"

Harri leaned back in her chair. Those were very good questions. Why the hell would Monica Reinhold even consider working with Trubble after everything he did to her? Harri met Susan's gaze. Time for a confession.

"Honestly, one of my worries when Miss Purrception surrendered was she planned to kill Trubble in prison." She took a sip of her cinnamon coffee. "But she's never struck me as being that stupid."

"True. If she killed him inside the prison, she'd be lucky to only get a life sentence with her extensive record," Aisha growled while she closed the office door and stalked across Harri's office with her cup of pixie barf. Even worse, Aisha was back to wearing her designer stilettos now that she was no longer pregnant. The damn things poked holes in Harri's perfectly vacuumed carpet.

"Therefore, she has to get Trubble out of the prison," Susan continued. "Kill him somewhere else and dispose of the body."

"And how's she going to do that?" Harri asked. "Black Death is tagging along as Trubble's bodyguard."

"That's what Hard Knock is for." Aisha sat down in the other visitor chair. "He distracts Black Death. Miss Purrception takes care of Trubble."

"That's . . ." Harri stared out her window. Vehicle and pedestrian traffic had picked up along 6th Street over the past year. Rey had become a community leader in the Canyon Block neighborhood in ways Tim couldn't in his grief over his family.

Maybe she'd bought into the kid's natural optimism. Part of her wanted to believe Miss Purrception was trying to change. Without her, Aisha wouldn't have been able to save Rey last year. Professor Paranoia would have used Rey to kill Aisha and her unborn child.

Most of all, Harri wanted to believe for Rue Liberty's sake. The retired superhero deserved to see her daughter become something other than a notorious supervillain. And Sourpuss and Nix needed their mother.

Harri turned back to her partners. "That's a possibility. But what if something else is going on? Something bad enough Trubble and Monica would consider joining forces?"

"It's a possibility—" Susan started to admit.

"Who cares?" Aisha's voice rose, which wasn't like her. "We should be thinking about the firm. We represented a supervillain who has escaped. Do you have a clue of what kind of PR nightmare it's going to cause?"

"If we don't figure out what's going on and why, the lives of everyone in this building are in danger," Susan spat back.

"Do you want to quit?" Aisha's eyes narrowed. "You knew what you were getting yourself into when we offered you a partnership."

"Technically, you are my client, too," Susan snapped. "I don't want your superhero self going off half-cocked on a crusade to capture Miss Purrception when the real dangers are Trubble and Black Death. Or have you forgotten what happened at your wedding reception?"

Harri jumped to her feet and banged her fist on her desk. "Stop it! Both of you! It scares me when I'm the one being sane and reasonable, and both of you are losing it." She took a deep breath and released it while her partners were looking at her with their mouths hanging open.

"I'm sorry," Susan said softly. "You're right."

Aisha didn't look half as embarrassed as Susan. Instead, she quietly said, "Fine. What do you suggest? We'll be getting calls from reporters once this gets out."

Harri relaxed and sat back down. "Tell Nella and whoever else who calls we are cooperating fully with authorities, and how disappointed we are that Miss Purrception chose this course of action. Susan, can you start making discreet calls to our other clients? See if they can shake any info from their street sources."

Susan nodded.

"In the meantime, I'll call Carol Inunza and see if she caught any hint of what Miss Purrception planned," Harri said.

Susan cleared her throat. "Before we start dealing with the Miss Purrception mess, what did you say to Mother Defiant?"

"Only that I had to discuss taking her on as a client with the entire partnership." Harri made a face. "She was rather adamant about talking to you directly. She claimed she wanted to apologize."

Susan folded her arms and looked at the floor for a moment before she raised her head with an evil grin. "Thanks for making the bitch sweat."

"It was my pleasure." Harri grinned back before she turned to Aisha. "If we take her on, she's going to be a handful. Susan vastly undersold her bitchiness. And she's currently dating Blue Racer."

"Ouch." Aisha winced. "If they break up, or worse, get hitched, that's going to cause some major ethical issues. We already have enough of those on our collective plates."

"No shit," Susan muttered. "And I have no doubt she will use them against us."

"What did she say about a change in branding?" Aisha asked.

"She was a little resistant to it," Harri admitted. "She wanted to know if the suggestion was due to her faith."

"I tried to talk her into rebranding two years ago," Susan murmured. "I agree with Aisha though. Mother Defiant doesn't get that people view her the same as pop singers who cavort nearly naked with religious imagery in their performances."

"So, she really is that tone-deaf and not deliberately courting controversy?" Aisha asked.

"Yes," Harri and Susan said at the same time.

Aisha looked over at Susan. "What if we give her that chance to apologize to you, but at the same time, we're honest with her?"

"You mean get her to change her mind about hiring us so it seems like she's rejecting us?" Susan asked.

"If we coddle her now, she's just going to keep pushing us," Aisha said. "Tell her up front, brutally if we have to, we're not going to put up with any of her shit."

"Are you suggesting a trial period?" Harri said.

"I wasn't, but that's not a bad idea." Aisha looked at her thoughtfully.

"So a full partnership meeting with her?" Susan asked.

"It's an excuse to write off a dinner at Nolan's." Harri grinned.

"All right," Susan said. "But not until Thursday. Make her sweat a couple of days."

"I was actually thinking of calling her on Friday," Harri confessed.

The intercom buzzed and Harri pressed the appropriate button. "Yes?"

Patty sighed. "Nella Lopez is on line one."

"And that's my cue." Aisha stood. "I'll call Blue Racer, too. See if I can't get more of a feel for what we need to do to make any relationship with Mother Defiant work."

"Aisha?" Harri called.

She turned around to face Harri. "Yeah?"

"Don't take off without letting me or Susan know."

"If I get a lead, no promises." Aisha whirled and stomped out of Harri's office, which meant she was concentrating to keep from floating through the reception area. Flying had become her default setting since she got her superpowers.

Susan waited a few seconds before she said softly, "That's a disaster waiting to happen."

"If we end the day with only one actual disaster and one potential disaster, we're batting better than usual," Harri answered.

Susan stood and pointed at her fancy computer watch. "Girl, it's not even ten a.m. yet. Given this firm's past performance, we'll be hitting a thousand for disasters by happy hour."

CHAPTER 4

Aisha sat at her desk and inhaled deeply in an attempt to compose herself. She hated to admit this to the others, but Miss Purrception's actions felt like a very personal stab in the back. Especially after everything they went through together last year against Professor Paranoia in Japan. She'd backed Rey and Captain Takashi Takeda of Japan's Superhuman Enforcement Bureau against Takeda's supervisors over releasing Miss Purrception because of her help. When Harri said Monica wanted to turn herself in, Aisha thought maybe Rey's pep talk had gotten through to the supervillain.

The little light on the Line 1 button blinked at Aisha accusingly. She had been thoroughly deceived, not by Miss Purrception, but by her own wishful thinking. That couldn't happen again. Not if she really wanted to continue as the new Ghost Owl.

She released the lungful of air, picked up her receiver, and tapped the button on the phone set. "Good morning, Nella. I'm assuming you want an official statement concerning Miss Purrception's escape."

The change of dialogue threw off the Action 12! News producer from her stammering. "Uh, y-yes. Are things that bad, Aisha? You usually make me dance a little bit before giving me the sound bite."

"Is that what you want? Me on camera for the statement?"

Nella chuckled. "You know I always want you on camera, girl! Do you have any idea how much our viewership goes up when you make an appearance? People in this city like you. In fact, I was hoping to have lunch with you this afternoon if you're free."

"Lunch?" Aisha could feel a hole about to open up beneath her feet. "May I ask why?"

"The station would like to offer you a job as an on-air legal commentator," Nella said.

"What?" The word exploded from Aisha's mouth.

"Come down to the station at eleven. We'll film your statement about the Mauvaises escape for the eleven news segment. Then we'll discuss what the station would like to do."

"What happened to Howard Dewey?" Aisha's former boss had been the station's on-air legal commentator since she had been in high school.

"His contract was up," Nella said. "The corporate overlords want someone younger and more representative of the citizens of Canyon Pointe."

"Uh-huh," Aisha drawled. "What really happened?"

"The asshole got handsy with Essie."

Rage surged through Aisha. Essie Morales, the evening co-anchor, was a sweet kid and damn good at her job. "Is Essie okay?"

"She's fine. Nothing a swift kick in the sack couldn't handle." Nella chuckled.

"You know he'll sue the shit out of the station for assault," Aisha said.

"He threatened to." Nella laughed some more. "Until we sent him a copy of the tape. Bob hadn't turned off his camera and caught the whole damn incident. Anyway, you were the first lawyer I pitched to our station manager as a replacement, and Mark said yes."

The silence dragged on for a second or two before Nella added, "The tab's on the station for lunch, and I told them I'd have to take you someplace nice like Nolan's."

Aisha glanced at the little clock in the corner of her computer monitor screen. "You're not giving me much time to prepare a statement."

"We both know what you're going to say, Aisha," Nella chided. "Hell, I could write your press release for you if you want. But I have a second favor to ask."

"I'm still not sure about the first favor."

"Can you get the Ghost Owl to make a formal statement on behalf of the supers' community about what they're doing to find Miss Purrception?"

Aisha's heart skipped a beat. Did Nella know the truth about Aisha and her alter ego? Had someone at the NSB leaked the information? Was the Corvus mole at the federal agency trying to cause more trouble for her and Rey after Trubble ended up in prison?

She swallowed hard. "I would have to call and ask. Can I ask why the Owl and not one of our other clients?"

"Because the Owl polled the highest in trust by our viewers," Nella said. "He's carrying a lot of leftover goodwill from his predecessor."

"But why?" Aisha protested. "The first Ghost Owl was a vigilante."

"And people think the new Owl is following in his daddy's footsteps," Nella said. "A chunk of them also think the new Owl got away with murdering Doctor Liquidation."

"The Ghost Owl did not murder anyone," Aisha growled. Is this what the public really thought of her? Tim had deliberately let stories foster about him as the original Ghost Owl, but he needed the bad ass reputation since he wasn't a super.

"Hey, I believe you." Nella sighed. "But the general public has a tendency to make up their own shit. In a way, it makes sense. The original Owl was on the little guys' side on the north end without following the normal rules of superheroing. So, in their minds, most the citizenry would believe the new Owl plays fast and loose with the rules, too."

"I can't hide this information from the new Owl, Nella, not without breaching my duty to a client." With her agitation between Miss Purrception's escape and the information on how the public looked at the Ghost Owl, Aisha's butt left her chair. She quickly hooked her toes under the roller arms of her seat, but even the chair wobbled, threatening to float into the air with her.

"Do what you have to, but if he won't do it, Sparx is our next choice," Nella said.

"I may be a few minutes late to the station with all the phone calls I'll need to make." Aisha grabbed the lip of her desk to keep her chair's wheels on the carpet. Just when she thought she could open the damn blinds in the morning again.

"No worries," Nella said cheerfully. "See you when you get here."

The line went dead, and Aisha slowly replaced the receiver in its cradle. Harri was going to go ballistic when she heard this news. Aisha took a long drink of her luke-warm peppermint mocha. It had cooled quite a bit more than she realized when she had been in Harri's office.

The intercom buzzed. Aisha set her mug on Tim's warmer and pressed the heating button. "Yeah, Patty?"

"Blue Racer is on line two," Patty said. "And just to warn you, he's pissed as hell. He wouldn't tell me what it was about, but I can guess."

Well, Mother Defiant didn't waste any time bitching to her boyfriend.

"Thanks, Patty. I'll handle it."

Aisha concentrated before she stood and closed her blinds. This wasn't going to be a fun conversation, and she didn't need any passersby witnessing her powers if she lost her temper. She carefully sat on her chair again, lifted the receiver, and pressed the blinking Line 2 button.

"Good morning, Blue Racer."

"Franklin, why the hell aren't you taking Mother Defiant on as a client?" the superhero shouted. "I personally vouched for you—"

"Stop right there," Aisha snapped. "First, she has been neither declined nor accepted as a client. Harri literally finished the intake interview less than an hour ago. Second, I told you from the start none of us can discuss any representation of her with you. If we do decline her, we will tell the reasons so to her face. Not to you. Third, we been a little busy this morning with things that have nothing to do with her or you."

"Sorry, I guess—" Air whistled through the phone's ear piece. "I thought it would be a slam dunk with me as a character witness."

"Racer, you should have told us you were seeing her socially," Aisha said gently.

"Oh, she told you about that?"

"Yes," Aisha continued. "It raises ethical concerns for us as a firm. There's also the fact she automatically assumed Susan Kennedy would want her back as a client. Plus, she walked into our building with all kinds of malware on her phone, including a bug from Corvus."

"I-I thought everyone from Corvus was in prison," Blue Racer said.

"Not all of them," Aisha said crisply. "What exactly did Mother Defiant say to you?"

"Just that she thought she really boffed the interview and Ms. Winters didn't seem to like her."

"You know how Harri is, Racer." Aisha pinched her leg to keep from laughing at the absurdity of the situation. "She isn't going to play the bullshit game, and if Mother Defiant came in here with a diva attitude, you know Harri would shut her down. Harri doesn't even put up with crap from Ultramegaperson. Mother Defiant sure isn't getting a pass. Hell, I'm going to have to tell Harri about this conversation, and that'll be a checkmark with her against Mother Defiant."

Blue Racer sighed. "Okay, I get it. I'm sorry I blew up at you, Aisha."

"Apology accepted." Aisha relaxed a little in her chair. "Was there anything else you needed?"

"No," he said meekly. "I'll talk to you later."

Aisha hung up, rested her forearms on her desk, and laid her head on top of them. Normal business things didn't get to her, but today had been a huge exception. What she really wanted to do was start searching for Miss Purrception. Tim was creating a search algorithm to compare and contrast the four escapees, and hopefully analyze what their next step might be.

Instead, Aisha had more meetings to deal with as Miss Purrception's attorney. And the first thing, she needed to do was inform her husband about the escape before he saw it on the news.

CHAPTER 5

Harri punched in the number for Carol Inunza as soon as Susan closed the office door on her way out. The phone rang twice before the receptionist answered.

"Inunza and Cervantes, how may I help you?"

"Good morning, Ngoc," Harri said as she played with her pen. "This is Harri Winters. Is Carol in?"

"One moment, Ms. Winters." Ngoc was nothing if not efficient.

The line clicked and Carol's teasing voice blasted through the speaker. "I expected your call before the NSB's, Harri."

"I'm surprised I haven't gotten a call from them yet about the escape." She frowned. It was weird. Carol was listed as second chair on all the legal documents regarding Miss Purrception. Why did the NSB call her first?

"Don't sweat it," Carol said. "It's probably because I was the last one to visit Miss Purrception at Mauvaises. If the NSB hasn't called you yet, how'd you find out?"

"I got a nasty call from my ex-husband this morning." Harri sighed. "Did you have any indication she planned something like this?"

"Probably about as much as you did. I brought up the fact she has a history of escaping custody with you at the beginning of our representation of her."

"Like I haven't gotten enough we-told-you-so's from my partners and staff this morning. Shit." Harri wanted to bang her head on her desk. "I really thought she was serious about turning a new leaf. This is going to break her family's hearts."

"I know it hurts putting your neck out like that," Carol crooned. "But all you can do is chalk it up to lesson learned."

"Did the NSB tell you who escaped with Miss Purrception?" Harri asked.

"Hard Knock, but those two are like peanut butter and jelly when it comes to jail breaks," Carol said with a laugh.

"Is that all they told you?" Harri could feel something was wrong. Why would the NSB hold back information with Carol? Unless the Corvus ally at the bureau was fishing for something.

"Harri, I'm too busy to play Twenty Questions, and so are you."

"Trubble and Black Death escaped with Purrception and Knock."

There was silence at the other end of the line. Long enough, Harri said, "Carol, talk to me. What are you thinking?"

Carol muttered an obscenity. "I'm thinking Miss Purrception is in over her head, and we're all in deep shit. Why the hell would she go off with that scumbag after everything he put her through?"

"She may not have had a choice in the matter," Harri said. "What if Black Death threatened her?"

"With what?" Carol asked. "If he killed her inside the prison, there is no way he'd ever get free. He'd be sedated until the day of his execution."

"We know we didn't uncover all of Corvus." Harri stopped tapping her pen. "If Trubble has been in contact with someone on the outside—"

"Threatening her family would be right up the bastard's alley," Carol finished. "Can you get them to safety? Do you need my help with anything?"

"No, I can take care of it," Harri murmured. "Thanks for your assistance, Carol."

God knew Harri didn't want to make this phone call, but Rue Liberty needed to know what had happened. Harri also knew she probably should be doing this in person, but Kerry and Molly lived with their grandmother, and she couldn't deal with the looks of disappointment on the young women's faces. She had seen the same look in her own mirror every time Dad fell off the wagon.

Harri gulped some more cinnamon coffee before she dialed the home number for Rue Liberty.

"Good morning, Harri." The retired superhero sounded as chipper as ever despite her advanced years.

"Hey, Rue. How's everything going?"

"Just wonderful with your investment tips." Rue chuckled. "But since I already RSVP'd to your Fourth of July party, want to tell me the real reason for this phone call?"

"Honestly, no, I don't," Harri said. "But there's something you should know. Monica escaped from prison last night. You may be getting a call from the NSB some time today."

The silence on the phone carried on for so long Harri feared she'd given the old lady a heart attack. "Rue, are you okay?"

"I—" Rue cleared her throat. "I want to say I'm surprised, but I'm not."

"I think we all wanted to believe Monica had turned the proverbial new leaf," Harri murmured. "Are the girls at home?"

"Kerry's at the Museum of Natural History with her girlfriend, and Molly just left. She needed to run an errand before she went to the Lechuza Building."

Of course, Molly was on her way here. Rey and Aisha hired Molly because they wanted another super to watch their baby, Harri's godson Mitch, for the five hours they were both at work.

Harri squeezed her eyes shut. She just needed to hide in her office until Molly went up to Aisha's loft. No, that was a chicken shit way to deal with the problem, and it sure as hell wasn't fair to Molly Reinhold, AKA the superhero Nix.

"I'll tell Molly what happened when she arrives." Harri hesitated. The last thing she wanted to do was ruin Kerry's date. "Do you know when—"

"I'll tell Kerry when she gets home." Rue sighed. "Provided the NSB doesn't pick her up before I talk her."

"None of you have to talk to them without legal counsel present, Rue," Harri said.

"I'm going to tell them the same thing I'm telling you now," Rue stated. "The last time I saw my daughter was the day of her sentencing. She asked me not to visit her in prison, and I haven't."

Harri winced. Talk about guilt. It sounded like both she and Rue Liberty had enough to coat the entire world. "I'm sorry to lay this on you—"

"Harri, you tried your best," Rue said.

"Yeah, but obviously my best wasn't good enough," Harri replied bitterly.

"It's worse when you're Miss Purrception's mother." Rue's laugh was equally bitter.

No sooner had Harri hung up the receiver when Patty buzzed her.

"I'm a little busy, Patty. Can you take a message?"

"Harri, Special Agent Wilbur Nesmith of the NSB is at the door." Patty's voice shook. "And he says he has a search warrant."

"Be right there." Harri resisted the urge to throw her phone and gently set the receiver in its cradle. For a Tuesday, this was beginning to feel like the worst Monday on record.

Chapter 6

Aisha flew up the stairwell to burn off some tension from this morning's chaos. She touched down on the fifth floor landing and opened the door to the hallway. However, the tension grew again as she approached her loft door. She punched in her security code. At the green light and beep, she rolled the door open.

Part of the tension melted away at the sight of Rey and Mitch sprawled on the baby's quilted play mat. Rey grinned up at Aisha.

"Hey, Mitch, let's show Mommy what you can do!"

For a split second, fear ripped through Aisha that her son had developed a superpower. Instead, Mitch grabbed Rey's outstretched fingers and pulled himself into a sitting position. The baby giggled and let go only to topple over, which made Mitch laugh harder.

Aisha released the air caught in her lungs. Normal infant development. Mitch was just three days past his fifth month. Of course, he was trying to sit up.

"That's amazing!" She laughed and clapped.

"You're a little early for lunch." Rey picked up Mitch and rolled to his feet.

"We need to talk, baby," she said.

"This sounds serious—hey!" Rey tried to disengage Mitch's tiny fist from his glossy black, longish hair.

"And you wondered why I had Jeremy hack off my dreds." Aisha grinned. Rey had been letting his hair grow out. Just one more way to differentiate himself from his twin brother Steve, even though the two men didn't find out about each other until last year.

"Take him a sec." Rey handed the baby to Aisha so he could pick up the play quilt and fold it. "Whatever it is, you don't have that panicked look, which means I don't have to suit up."

Aisha sighed. "Maybe we will before the day is over. Miss Purrception escaped from Mauvaises last night."

Rey paused as he was about to toss the quilt on their casual padded arm chair that matched their relatively new couch. He muttered an obscenity as he completed the action.

"Hey! Not in front of Mitch." Aisha covered the baby's ears.

Rey shot her a sour look. "Like his godmother isn't going to teach him the words you can't say on radio and TV?" He shook his head and stared out the huge industrial-style windows of their loft. "I thought she was serious about reforming."

"So was I, baby," Aisha murmured. "So was I. But it gets worse. She broke out with Trubble and Black Death."

"That doesn't make any sense." Rey shook his head. "Trubble's the reason she lost custody of Kerry and Molly years ago. She wouldn't help him if her life depended it."

"Did she ever say anything to you about Hard Knock?"

Rey shook his head again. "Not specifically, but then, she has contacts all over the world. I take it he was part of the jail break."

"Yeah." Aisha looked down at Mitch. If anyone tried to take him, she'd fight tooth and nail. "Maybe Susan's right."

"Susan's right about what?" Rey asked.

"She suggested Miss Purrfection played Trubble to get him out of the prison, so she could kill him and hide the body."

Rey said nothing. He padded to the kitchen area on his bare feet, opened the fridge, and started pulling out items to make lunch. Normally, Aisha wouldn't interrupt his culinary efforts, but his silence was worrisome.

"Rey? Baby?" Aisha carried Mitch to the island counter that separated the kitchen from the living room. "Talk to me."

He turned to face her. "What do you want me to say? Monica's not capable of killing? We both know she's capable of anything if she thinks it's in her best interest." He ran his hands through his hair. "What the hell do we say to Molly when she gets here?"

Damn. Aisha closed her eyes. She'd been so wrapped up in her own hurt feelings it hadn't registered how this would affect Nix, Sourpuss, or Rue Liberty.

Mitch started fussing. She opened her eyes and jiggled him. "I guess he's ready for lunch early."

"The appearance of Mommy does usually signal its meal time." Rey chuckled, but he quickly sobered. "I should be out there looking for her."

"Before you go off half-cocked, Tim's working on a tracking algorithm." Aisha walked over to their breakfast table and grabbed the nursing pillow. "We need to know where to look." She turned to look at her husband. "Unless you know any of her local contacts?"

"Only Rue and the girls." Rey snickered. "And Tim."

"Do not be saying that in front of Harri," Aisha said. "And technically, you qualify as one of Miss Purrception's local contacts, too."

"Hey!" Rey protested. "I wasn't doing the rooftop rumba with her like Tim was."

"No one said you were, but for Mitch's sake, if she contacts you, let me know."

"Mitch's sake?" Rey looked up from the bread he was buttering for grilled ham and gouda.

Aisha sighed. "I don't want his daddy to end up in Mauvaises for aiding and abetting a fugitive."

"Cross my heart—" Rey crossed himself with the knife still in his hand. "I will tell you if Miss Purrception even tries to contact me."

"You damn well better, Reyes Garcia, or it won't be the NSB you have to worry about," Aisha growled.

CHAPTER 7

Harri stomped out of her office and over to Patty's desk. Both sets of the front doors were locked. Patty didn't buzz anyone in unless it was someone with an appointment. After the rash of murder attempts on all the partners last year, it wasn't worth anyone's lives trying to act like a normal law firm.

Patty gestured at the man waiting outside the first set of doors.

NSB Agent Wilbur Nesmith was easily in his mid-sixties. He was roughly six-two with a full head of salt-and-pepper hair. He also reminded Harri of a kids' show host from her own childhood with his patient air. Aisha was right. Nesmith looked like someone's kindly next-door neighbor instead of a kick-ass fed. They couldn't underestimate him.

Harri strode down the steps, through the second set of doors, and out the first. Hot summer air hit her skin like a blast furnace. "You can't search an attorney's office without a hell of a case or a real dumbass judge. Let me see the warrant." She held out her palm.

"And good morning to you, too, Ms. Winters." Nesmith smiled genially while he pulled out the paperwork from his inner suit pocket.

Harri yanked it from his hand and took her dear sweet time scanning the warrant before she looked up at him. "Are you kidding me?"

"NSB agents never kid, Ms. Winters," he said. "I'm sure Ms. Franklin can attest to that."

"She also told me you like to leave your partner in the car with the windows cracked. Do I need to get him water and a treat?"

"Actually, he decided to get a mani-pedi while I spoke with you." Nesmith gestured at the nail salon down the street.

Harri narrowed her eyes. "It's going to take you twice as long doing a search by yourself. Not to mention, if Miss Purrception were really here, we'd just move her to one of the law offices. So, why are you putting my partner's husband on the spot?"

Nesmith stepped closer and lowered his voice. "I'm hoping Black Falcon cooperates with me in order to keep his friend alive."

Harri could feel her blood pressure rising. He knew Rey's secret identity. Of course, Nesmith knew. He was freaking NSB. "You really believe he would help her?"

The agent shrugged. "I have to pursue all potential leads, Ms. Winters. You understand, of course."

She folded her arms over her chest and tapped her right toe on the concrete. "I also understand that someone in the NSB set him up to be captured by Professor Paranoia."

"Really? I was under the impression it was Captain Justice who was captured by Professor Paranoia, and he's dead," Nesmith replied.

The implicit threat pissed Harri off, but now was not the time, and the sidewalk in front of her law office was not the place. "Fine. You win." She motioned for Patty to unlock the door. "For now."

The door's lock hummed and clicked. Harri held the door for Nesmith. He smirked and entered. The first door swung shut, and another hum filled the small space between the double doors, but he didn't mention it or ask what caused the noise.

Good. He wasn't going to treat her like she was stupid.

Patty's voice filtered through the intercom. "He's clean, Harri."

For some strange reason, that surprised her. She looked up at Nesmith. "Not even a gun?"

He shrugged. "What good would it do with all the supers who live here? Besides, you've taken out how many Corvus agents by yourself without weapons, and you're not even a super."

She couldn't show how many brownie points Nesmith earned with that assessment. Ignoring his flattery, she growled to Patty, "Have Tim meet us in reception, please."

"Yes, ma'am."

If Patty had called Harri "ma'am" any other time, she would have been poking at Harri's attitude. This time, their assistant was incredibly serious.

The second set of doors hummed and clicked. Harri yanked the right door open. Nesmith followed her up the steps to the foyer of the original building that they turned into Patty's domain. The antique elevator grumbled to halt, and Tim strode around the corner in reception.

"What's going—" He caught sight of Nesmith and finished with "Oh."

Tim turned to Patty. "Did you scan—"

"Yes." Her tone was brittle, and she didn't take her eyes off of the NSB agent.

"Agent Nesmith has a warrant to search Rey and Aisha's loft," Harri bit out.

Tim picked up her message to play good cop. He bestowed a gracious smile upon Nesmith and gestured toward the elevator. "All right. This way, please, Special Agent Nesmith."

Harri looked at Patty, who merely nodded. Their assistant would call upstairs and warn Aisha of the incoming cow cookie. Harri trudged after Tim and Nesmith toward the elevator. This was a runaround of the law office, and she damn well knew it. She just prayed Aisha didn't have any firm materials in her loft, and if she did, she'd get it out of her loft with Patty's warning. All three partners had a tendency to take work home with them, even if home was a few stories above their offices.

Tim closed the gates behind her, and the elevator slowly rose up the shaft. She should have made the damn NSB agent climb the four flights of stairs.

When they reached the top floor, Tim opened the gates and beckoned Nesmith to follow him. "This way, Special Agent."

"I think I could have found Garcia's apartment by myself," Nesmith said.

"No one wanders around our building unescorted," Tim stated coolly as they walked down the hall. "Not with all the crap Corvus has pulled."

"That's amusing coming from an accused murderer," Nesmith said.

"What part of 'crap Corvus has pulled' do you not understand, Special Agent?" Harri snapped. "They get off on kidnapping, hurting, and murdering children, including the son of my head of security."

Nesmith stopped in midstride and pivoted to glare at Harri. "I'm not part of Corvus, Ms. Winters."

"We don't know that for sure, so we take precautions because we have children living in this building." She shot him a vicious smile. "You understand, of course."

After a long pause, he inclined his head. "Yes, I do."

Tim knocked on Aisha and Rey's door. It immediately slid back. Rey's bearded mug didn't have his customary smile, but he nodded politely. Harri still had problems with how mature he looked now compared to the nervous kid he had been when she first met him.

"Special Agent Nesmith, please come in." Rey stepped to the side to allow his guests to enter.

Nesmith entered the loft and hesitated in mid-step. When Harri followed him inside, she saw why. Aisha sat on the couch while breastfeeding Mitch, not even bothering with a cover. It was all Harri could do not to bust out laughing. If Nesmith said a damn word, Aisha would scream sex discrimination faster than she could fly. She was in her own damn home after all.

"Uh, Mr. Garcia, um, well . . ." Nesmith tried hard to look everywhere but at the couch.

"Special Agent Nesmith has a warrant to search your home including all your belongings, Rey," Harri said. "I suggest you cooperate."

Nesmith stepped forward to start his search, but Harri said, "Aisha, you got anything from the firm up here that you were working on?"

"No," she said with just a hint of a smile. "Everything is in the law office." Which meant anything she did have in here was now sitting in Harri's loft, and the warrant specifically listed only Rey and Aisha's place.

Nesmith's gaze moved from Harri to Aisha and back before he exhaled wearily. "Can't we at least try to be cordial here?"

"You should have thought of that before you requested the warrant," Harri said.

Nesmith sighed again before he pulled a notebook and pen out of his suit jacket pocket. "Mr. Garcia, when was the last time you spoke with Monica Reinhold, AKA Miss Purrception?"

"Don't answer that!" Harri and Aisha yelled at the same time.

Mitch burbled something that sounded like, "Yeah," before he returned to sucking away at his lunch.

"Let me see the warrant, Harri." Aisha waggled her fingers.

Harri examined her best friend as she crossed the room. Superhero. New mom. And damn if her nails weren't perfectly filed and polished. How had their friendship lasted this long?

Aisha took the warrant with her free hand and read it. She glared at Nesmith. "This warrant says nothing about taking my husband into custody for questioning or subpoenaing a statement from him."

Nesmith turned to Rey who leaned against the rough brick wall with his arms crossed. "It's in your best interests to cooperate, Black Falcon."

"Or what?" Rey's sly smile resembled his twin brother Steve's, which sent a chill through Harri. For the umpteenth time, she wondered if she hadn't made a huge mistake by promising the street kid she would make him rich by turning him into a legitimate superhero.

"You'll drug me, torture me, and leave me on an abandoned oil derrick in the middle of the Indian Ocean while trying to kill my wife and son?" Rey continued.

Nesmith's jaw worked as he considered what to say. Finally, he ground out, "Point taken. I'll search your place per the terms of the warrant."

Harri and Aisha exchanged looks while Nesmith poked around the living area. The only things big enough to hold a person were Mitch's playpen and toy box. The NSB agent paused to examine the titles of books on the shelves that covered the entire south wall of the loft, before he shuffled into the kitchen, opened and closed cupboards, and checked the fridge.

Tim followed Nesmith into the rest of the loft containing two bedrooms, a full bath, and the couples' home office. Even Harri could hear him searching through closets and drawers.

Mitch burbled, and Aisha murmured, "Could you hold him for a sec, Harri?"

"Hey, there, big guy!" She threw the burping towel Aisha handed her over her shoulder, placed Mitch on top of the towel, and gently patted his back. "Oof! What are you guys feeding this kid?"

"He was in the ninety-ninth percentile at his last well baby check-up." Aisha said. "Doctor O'Brien thinks he might grow taller than Rey."

"Then we need to step up our licensing game," Harri muttered. "Ordering specialty sizes will be a pain in the ass, not to mention expensive as hell."

"I think we can manage," Rey said.

Oops. Harri glanced at Aisha who grimaced as she cleaned up and put her clothes back in place.

"I think your Aunt Harri stepped in something," Harri murmured to Mitch. He responded with a pretty loud belch for a baby.

"I need to get down to the Action 12! studios," Aisha said. "Can you handle—" She inclined her head in the direction of the voices on the other side of the loft.

"I promise not to let Rey hang Agent Nesmith from the Del Oro Bank tower antenna." Harri grinned at Rey.

"And I promise to listen to my attorneys," Rey added.

"Great." Aisha stood up and grabbed her oversized purse. "I don't have time today to go downtown and bail you two out." She bent and pecked Mitch on the head before she strode over to Rey and gave him a much more adult kiss. "I'll be back in a couple of hours." She walked out of the loft at a fast pace. If there was one thing Aisha hated, it was being late.

Unless it was getting to her own office on time. She never hid that she wasn't much of a morning person. Harri had worried about her best friend taking a lackadaisical approach to their own business, but other than a brief bout of morning sickness, Aisha was in her office by nine a.m. every morning.

A few seconds later, Tim escorted Agent Nesmith back to the living room area.

"One last thing, Mr. Garcia," Nesmith said. "I need to see your phone."

Rey frowned and looked at Harri.

Unfortunately, the phone was listed on the warrant currently sitting on the coffee table where Aisha had tossed it after she read it. Harri nodded. "Unlock it."

Rey pulled the phone out of his jeans pocket and tapped in his code before he held it out for Nesmith. However, Nesmith typed something on the device and handed it back almost immediately. Rey's frown deepened before he brought it over to show Harri.

On the notepad app, Nesmith had typed:

Do you have a jammer so we can talk privately?

"Hey, Tim, can you hold our godson for a minute?" she said.

Tim walked over, and she handed him Rey's phone. His frown matched Rey's expression.

"Is there anything else before we go back downstairs, Agent Nesmith?" Tim said at the same time he nodded.

"No, that pretty much covers it," the NSB agent said pleasantly.

Tim tossed Rey's phone back to the kid and pulled one of his inventions out of the pocket of his tan twill trousers. He thumbed a switch.

"Patty scanned you when you came in," Harri said.

"You have a signal router for your own cell phones to work inside the building," Nesmith said. "The Justice Department has figured out how to send a signal through that router."

"Don't you mean the NSB?" Harri said.

Nesmith shook his head. "Ms. Winters, you don't realize how many enemies you made when you brought down Corvus. Attorney General Dowdy got cocky when he confronted you in San Francisco last month. And he suddenly closed his exploration committee regarding running for president. So someone, somewhere along the way lowered the hammer on him. The warrant is because you're on his shit list for losing the possible nomination." He faced Rey. "I'm sorry you got caught in the middle of this, Mr. Garcia, but you were the only contact outside of Miss Purr-ception's family and attorneys here in the U.S."

Rey's right eyebrow rose. "What about her supervillain contacts?"

"Surprisingly, she doesn't have many in this country outside of Hard Knock," Nesmith said. "That's why Assistant U.S. Attorney Richards pushed that damn search warrant through with the judge."

"Richards?" Harri said. "Phillip Richards?"

Nesmith cocked his head. "You know him?"

Harri scowled at the agent. "He was second chair during Ultramegaperson's arraignment last month." The trans superhero had a major attitude, but they knew their fans and audience. Better yet, they'd never had a casualty in their twenty-year career.

Which made the feds blaming them for the destruction of the north end of the Golden Gate Bridge and subsequent deaths all the more suspicious. The first chair prosecutor at the arraignment Derek Jamison was a young, fresh-out-of-law-school kid looking to make his mark on the world. Richards was older and pretty damn quiet. In fact, Harri had been surprised their roles hadn't been reversed, which had set off her own internal alarms during Ultramegaperson's arraignment.

"Why are you talking to us?" Harri asked the NSB agent in front of her.

"Because someone's using my agency to harm supers." Nesmith gestured toward Rey. "You aren't the only one, Black Falcon. Plus, Corvus used the Federal Supers Academy to recruit a lot of their agents. Two students disappeared last week. We believe someone's trying to pick up where Corvus left off."

Kids disappearing from federal custody didn't bode well. It wasn't like the academy was a voluntary school. These were the kids either surrendered by their parents because they couldn't handle a child with powers or taken by the government because the children were deemed too dangerous to be in public. Black Death had been one of those kids. Even more worrisome, no alerts had gone out about the missing kids. Not even through the law enforcement agencies.

But hell, if Nesmith wanted to talk, Harri would milk as much out of him as she possibly could.

"The creeps who tried to kill us in San Francisco, Doctor Liquidation, and Gil Wilcrest were all trying to find the original Ghost Owl," Harri said. "How the hell did a rumor get started that he's still alive?"

Nesmith shrugged. "Unfortunately, it was your man Drallhickey's stunt in court during his girlfriend's custody hearing. The rest of the witnesses and gallery doing their Spartacus stunt meant you all are protecting the original Ghost Owl. The scuttlebutt making the rounds on the streets is the new G.O. is the original's son." He smiled. "Even though we all know that's not true."

He jammed his hands into his trouser pockets. "I thought not arresting Harper Collins when she was here would convince Ms. Franklin and Ms. Kennedy to trust me. We want the same things, Ms. Winters. To root out the remainder of Corvus and the people who enabled Byron Trubble. He needs to be in prison."

"Prove it. Do you have any leads of where he and Black Death may go next?" Harri asked.

"No." Nesmith shook his head. "I know you can't tell me because you're Miss Purrception's attorney." He looked at Rey. "I was hoping you might confide in me about any places she may go."

"If you'd asked when I was Captain Justice, I would have," Rey said. "But I was also a naïve idiot who thought everything was black and white. Now, I have no reason on earth to trust you."

"Besides," Tim said. "You have eyes on her mother and daughters already, don't you?"

Nesmith exhaled wearily. "And bugs on their phones." The agent turned to Tim. "You need to add an YK scrambler to your assembly to keep them from spying on you in here."

Tim looked surprised by the information. He immediately switched to his thinking face.

Nesmith turned back to Harri. "We know we have a mole connected to Corvus, but we haven't been able to find out who it is."

"You told Aisha that NSB's Internal Affairs believed Professor Paranoia used his powers on one of your people," Harri said.

"That's the official story, but the head of NSB believes otherwise."

Again, Nesmith shrugged. "I don't know what else to do to earn yours and your partners' trust, Ms. Winters. I want to clean up my bureau, and I know I can't do it alone."

He seemed sincere, but then, all the good con artists did. Harri shifted Mitch from her shoulder to her lap and wiped the milky drool from her godson's face.

"You're going to have to prove yourself, Nesmith." Harri held up her free index finger when he opened his mouth. "By actions." She held up the warrant. "Not by this type of shit, even though I know it takes a prosecutor to push it."

Nesmith's eyes narrowed. "You want me to be your informant in the NSB, like your ex-husband is for the FBI?"

Harri smirked. "It is ironic that that only law enforcement officer or prosecutor we trust to do the right things happen to be our ex-husbands."

Nesmith exhaled gustily. "Understood. Well, I need to get downstairs before my partner gets suspicious."

Tim pulled the loft door open and gestured for Nesmith to go first. Rey crossed the room and took Mitch from Harri.

"You okay," she asked softly.

"Yeah." He smiled at his son. "Just starting to feel a little picked on."

"I never meant—"

"Don't ever apologize, Harri." Rey's old, soft, shy smile was back. "I wouldn't have Aisha and Mitch in my life if you hadn't pushed me to go legit. To me, it's worth the annoyance people like Nesmith cause."

Harri hurried through the loft door after Tim and Nesmith. The rollers rumbled as Rey pulled the door closed.

Once Harri was inside the elevator and closed the gates, Tim turned off his device and stuck it in his pocket as they rode the car down. When the elevator ground to a halt on the first floor, Nesmith took that as his cue.

"I can't believe you use that death trap in a building with children as residents," he grumbled in a loud voice. "It's a hazard. Get it fixed, or get it replaced."

"Our maintenance man had it fixed in ten minutes," Tim shot back.

They continued the fake argument until Nesmith left the building. He passed Molly Reinhold on the sidewalk.

She entered her passcode at each door and jogged up the steps. "Did you know the guy who was just here is NSB?"

"Yes," Harri and Tim said.

"What's up?" Molly's fine raspberry-colored eyebrows formed a "V".

The conversation Harri hoped to shove off on Aisha roosted on her own plate.

"Molly, come into my office." Harri waved in the direction of her office door. "There's something I need to tell you before you go upstairs."

Chapter 8

◆━━◆●◆━━◆

Aisha wove in and out of traffic as she sped down Shoreline Drive. Whatever game Nesmith was playing, Harri could handle it.

She glanced at the clock. Shit. It was already after eleven, but she had warned Nella she'd be a few minutes late.

Funny how when she had an expensive sports car, other drivers would deliberately cut her off. But a mom in a minivan driving like a maniac? They got the hell out of the way.

Of course, it would have been faster to fly. How did other supers deal with day-to-day life without using their abilities? It had only been a little over a year since she developed HRSP. Now that her abilities were permanent, she found she wanted to use them more and more. It was something to ask Qiang about the next time she spoke with her.

If she asked Rey about it, he'd shake his head, laugh, and say, "If you want to fit in, you don't use your powers. I never fit in, so for me, it was simple survival to not use mine. You're lucky you already know how to blend in with everyone."

Aisha flipped the turn signal, pulled into the TV station's parking lot, and quickly found an open visitor's spot. She sucked in a deep breath of chilled air inside the minivan before she opened the driver-side door and stepped out of her vehicle. Despite all her vaunted powers, summer heat smacked her hard. Thanks to Lake Del Oro, Canyon Pointe wasn't suffering the one hundred-degree weather the rest of the state endured. But a five-degree difference didn't mean much when her makeup was melting off her face.

Ted Meadowfield's pearly whites shone down at Aisha from the billboard on the side of the building. Part of her wanted to poach Essie Morales from her current representation because the young reporter's face should be up there. Being the station owner's son-in-law was the only reason Ted hadn't been fired for his bullshit. The A/C blasting in the reception area of the station was Aisha's salvation.

The young man with raspberry tresses in a fashionable style sitting at the desk smiled at her. "How may I help you this fine day?"

"Aisha Franklin. I have an appointment with Nella Lopez."

Before he could answer, Essie popped out of the door to the inner sanctum. "I was beginning to worry you were going to blow us off."

"Sorry, I'm so late." Aisha flashed her professional smile as they shook hands. "It's been a rather hectic morning."

"I can understand." Essie released Aisha's hand and gestured for her to follow the reporter. "I've got Ms. Franklin, Luis."

"Okie-doke." He waggled his fingers.

Once they passed into the station's office area, Aisha murmured, "Another new receptionist?"

"Ted can't drive this one away." Essie giggled. "Luis is his nephew."

"Haley Riggs' son by a certain Hall of Fame pitcher with the Copperheads?"

"Yep."

The scandal had been a major topic in the city twenty-some years ago. Haley was the youngest daughter of Riley Riggs, the owner of both Canyon Pointe's largest TV station and the Copperheads. Getting knocked up at eighteen was one thing, but the truth came out during her wedding nuptials to Mark Thompson, the goalie for the Canyon Pointe Panthers.

Thompson and Jose Martinez had a knock-down, drag-out in the church when Jose interrupted the service to claim Haley was pregnant with his child. Haley refused to marry either man. Riggs disowned poor Haley. She retaliated with a tell-all book in order to feed and shelter her infant son. And the father and daughter only reconciled after Mrs. Riggs begged them on her deathbed.

There had even been a TV mini-series made based on the scandal.

Aisha chuckled. "That has to be blowing Ted's mind."

"Even better, Luis always calls him 'Uncle Ted.'" Essie's grin widened.

They entered the secondary news studio since the primary one was being used for Action 12!'s twenty-four-hour news channel. However, this studio was just as busy and maybe even a little noisier. The lighting made the room nearly as hot as the summer day outside. The camera people were lining up their equipment while the sound person was checking all the connections for the portable microphones.

Headphones on, Nella paused in issuing orders and walked over to Essie and Aisha. "This will go out on tonight's six o'clock broadcast—"

"Can we do it for the noon news broadcast instead?" Aisha asked.

Nella blinked. "Sure, but it'll have to be live. What changed your mind?"

"I can't tell you everything right now." Aisha sucked in a deep breath. "But the NSB is targeting a lot of people because of Miss Purrception."

"I did my research," Essie protested. "She doesn't have that many contacts in the U.S. And from what little I know, she has a legitimate gripe against the NSB for taking her children. She didn't go the villain route until they took her children away because she wouldn't tell them who their father was."

"That's true." Aisha eyed Nella. "But several of our clients are being treated as guilty by association by the NSB. I'd like to stand up for them and send out a personal plea for Miss Purrception to turn herself in."

"That would be a ratings boost," Essie said. "How long would you need?"

"Fifteen seconds," Aisha answered.

Essie turned to Nella. "I can trim my questions if you're okay with us not having time to rehearse."

Nella eyed them both before her shoulders sagged. "All right, but if you make me regret this, Franklin, I will sic Meadowfield on your ass."

"You won't." Aisha crossed her heart for good measure.

"Get over to makeup," Nella said to her. She pointed at Essie. "You've got five minutes to adjust your questions. And I want to see it before we go on air. This will be our top story." She walked away to arrange for the change in format for the noon hour.

Essie guided Aisha to the makeup artist Christa before the reporter trotted off to revise her notes.

"How's it going, Ms. Franklin?" Christa grinned as Aisha pulled her makeup bag from her tote and handed it to the makeup artist. "It's been a while since you've been in the studio."

"I've been a little busy with the new addition to the family." Aisha smiled back. She sat in the chair, and Christa whipped out a cape and covered Aisha's suit.

While Christa was a true professional, her predecessor had been jerk. Aisha started bringing in her own cosmetics because the jerk refused to carry anything for someone whose complexion was as dark as Aisha's.

She'd continued with Christa, both out of sheer habit and because the makeup artist pointed out Aisha bought better quality cosmetics than the station's budget would allow for.

"Please tell me you've got pics." Christa said. She pulled bottles and brushes from the case.

"Of course." Aisha pulled out her phone and showed photos of Mitch while Christa worked her magic.

"Damn, he is so adorable," Christa gushed. "He's going to be a heart-breaker just like his daddy. You're going to have a hard time keeping the girls away from Mitch."

Aisha shuddered. "Don't say that. I want to keep my precious baby for as long as possible."

"They grow faster than you know." Christa carefully removed the cape. "Heck, my oldest starts kindergarten this fall."

"Almost show time, people!" Nella clapped her hands, too, but her shout was enough to get everyone's attention in the studio.

The sound guy helped Aisha clip the microphone in place and tucked the battery pack onto her skirt's waistband. She could have done this in her sleep, but the guy was simply doing his job. He had her say a few test phrases to make sure the mike was working. She buttoned her suit jacket while she climbed the two steps to the set's carpeted platform.

The set consisted of two pleather arm chairs and an oval table be-tween and slightly behind the two seats. The table normally had a plant or flowers since this was the same set used for the local late afternoon talk show and the Sunday morning religious show. Today, there were no decorations on the table since this was a "serious" interview.

There was a lot of last minute shuffling. Lighting adjustments. Sound adjustments.

Essie looked as nervous as Aisha felt, and the reporter deliberately ignored her and stared at her notes on her lap. Behind the glare of the lights and bank of cameras, everyone went silent. Everyone, but the director who called out the countdown to air time.

When the director reached "1", Essie lifted her head and looked into the center camera, her serious journalist expression plastered to her face. "Welcome to Action 12! News Noon Edition. Today's top story, the escape of notorious supervillain Miss Purrception along with three other inmates from Mauvaises Prison last night. Here in the studio with us is Aisha Franklin of the Law Offices of Winters and Franklin, Miss Purrception's attorneys."

Essie shifted to face Aisha. "Thank you for coming, Ms. Franklin."

"I wish I could say it was a pleasure to be here," Aisha answered smoothly.

"Winters and Franklin is noted for its representation of superheroes, including the late, lamented Captain Justice," Essie started. "Why on earth is your firm representing Miss Purrception?"

"Last Christmas, Miss Purrception approached my partner about turning herself in," Aisha replied. "We truly believed she had repented and she wanted to be able to see her family, including her children, again. We would not have taken her as a client otherwise."

"Surely, Miss Purrception didn't think she would get off scot-free by simply turning herself in?" Essie glanced at her notes. "She's considered responsible for a multi-million dollar bank heist in Rio de Janeiro, a break-in at the Louvre where she allegedly stole, among other art, the Eros Medallion and the Mona Lisa, and here in the U.S., she is the prime suspect in the theft of the Declaration of Independence."

Aisha smiled. "I'm not defending any of her actions. However, the Declaration of Independence was returned."

"She left it in the bathroom of the president's private residence at the White House," Essie said with a slightly disgusted tone.

"Miss Purrception knew there would be consequences for her past acts." Aisha gestured matter-of-factly. "In fact, she's been a model prisoner at Mauvaises according to the reports we've received from the warden."

"What was the reaction of Carol Inunza of the Law Firm of Inunza and Cervantes?" Essie continued. "She is Miss Purrception's co-counsel."

"Harri Winters spoke with Ms. Inunza as soon as we found out what had happened." Aisha could feel her butt hover a millimeter above her chair. She squeezed her clasped hands together and focused on the discomfort to remain seated. Floating around the news set would be the worst thing that could happen today. "None of Miss Purrception's attorneys, including myself, had any indication she was about to break out."

"The NSB hasn't given an official statement yet. Have they spoken to you?"

Aisha resisted the urge to smile. Essie couldn't have done this better if they had planned it. "In fact, I spoke with Wilbur Nesmith, the NSB agent assigned to the case, just before I came to the studio. Another very dangerous super, Black Death, escaped with Miss Purrception and Hard Knock along with Byron S. Trubble."

"The retired general who was illegally running black ops by using supers?"

"Yes." Aisha nodded firmly. "Black Death was one of Trubble's top operatives at Corvus. We have reason to believe Miss Purrception and Hard Knock may not have been willing participants in the prison escape."

"What makes you say that?" Essie asked.

"Miss Purrception despises Trubble," Aisha said grimly. "She only turned to villainy after he manipulated the courts into taking her children from her."

"If you could talk to Miss Purrception right now, what would you say?" Essie finished.

Aisha faced the camera directly. "Miss Purrception, you asked Winters and Franklin to help you mend fences with your family and to turn over the proverbial new leaf. I'm asking, no, I'm pleading with you to turn yourself in. You know the NSB will take this out on your parents and your children if you don't surrender. If you are doing this under duress, your friends from Japan have your back."

She inhaled and added, "And I have a direct message from the Ghost Owl. 'I went out on a limb for you. Don't make me hunt you down. Because I will, and neither of us want the fall-out if I have to bring you in.'"

"Why does the Ghost Owl care about what happens to Miss Purrfection?" Essie asked.

Aisha gave her a mournful look. "No one knew about this outside of our firm and the parties involved, but with the original Jatz'om Kuh dead, the new Ghost Owl isn't hiding the truth anymore. A long time ago, Miss Purrception had an affair with the original Ghost Owl."

"A-are you saying the new Ghost Owl is the child of Miss Purrception and the original Ghost Owl?" Essie stared at Aisha with equal measures of surprise and triumph at getting the scoop of the decade.

"What child doesn't want their mother home safe and sound?" Aisha prayed Monica would get the message. If she didn't, Aisha would be forced to bring in her own damn client.

And a part of her still wanted the bitch's head on a pike.

CHAPTER 9

❖

Harri would have done almost anything not to have this conversation with Molly. Susan and Aisha were so much better at the touchy, feely crap. But the girl deserved to hear the news from a friendlier face than an NSB agent.

Maybe Nesmith was being honest about wanting to help the firm, and they assist him, in return, by tracking down the mole. He had to have known who Molly Reinhold was when he passed her on the sidewalk a few minutes ago.

Harri and Molly entered Harri's office. She waved toward the couches. "Have a seat."

"Just tell me what's going on." Molly crossed her arms over her chest. "I know it's not related to any of my licensing contracts. Aisha would have just called me."

"All right." Harri sucked in a deep breath. "Your mom broke out of Mauvaises Prison last night with Hard Knock, Black Death, and Byron Trubble."

Molly said nothing. Her expression turned to stone. She dropped her arms, crossed to Harri's couches, and sat gingerly on the closest one.

"Sweetie, can I get you something?" Concern rolled through Harri.

Molly laughed bitterly. "If I wasn't supposed to watch Mitch this afternoon, I'd ask for a couple of shots from the bottle of whiskey you keep in your credenza."

Harri walked over and sat beside the girl. "I know a place with great margaritas if you want to go out after we're both done with work."

"I might take you up on it." Molly released a deep breath. "Have you told Grandma yet?"

"Yes. She said you had just left to run an errand before you came here."

Molly turned to face Harri. "Does Kerry know yet?"

Harri shook her head. "I doubt it. Rue said she was out with her girl-friend. She didn't want to ruin their date."

"That sounds like Grandma." Molly flopped against the back of the couch. "Kerry's going to go on an I-told-you-so rant when she finds out."

"Oh, I already got that one from my partners." Harri chuckled. "I'll stop at the ATM. We're going to need a lot of tequila."

"Damn." Molly stared at the ceiling. A tear leaked from her eye and trickled down her temple and into her multi-colored hair. "I really thought she wanted to change."

"Sweetie, right now, you have no idea what's going on." Harri shook her head. "Neither do I. And it's awfully strange that your mom would break out with Trubble. He's the reason she lost custody of you and Kerry. She hates the bastard with a passion."

"Or so she says." Molly sniffed and wiped the moisture from her face before she sat upright.

"Have you forgotten what happened at Aisha and Rey's wedding?" Harri laid her hand on the girl's arm. "Black Death could have threatened your mom or—" God, she hated admitting this part. "—more likely Hard Knock. For all her faults, your mom does stick up for her friends."

"You don't have to remind me she chooses everyone else over her family," Molly said sourly.

"That's not what I meant." Harri grimaced. Maybe she should have left breaking the news to Molly to her partners. Hell, even Arthur could have done a better job than Harri did.

Molly stood. "Thanks for letting me know, but I need to get upstairs before Rey has to leave for the restaurant."

"The margarita offer is still open."

The young superhero nodded before she charged out of Harri's office. If Mitch was down for his nap, she'd be alone to have the good cry she obviously needed.

Harri leaned back and stared at the ceiling herself. She knew better than most what the kid was feeling right now. The last stupid thing her own father did was drive his sports car off a cliff while high on cocaine. After twenty-five years, the disappointment still ran thick.

"Harri?" Patty's voice was followed by a knock on the door.

"Come in," Harri called out.

Once again, her assistant burst into her office and grabbed the remote. "Aisha's on the noon news broadcast."

Harri sat upright. "I thought they were filming her segment for broadcast later tonight."

"That's what she told me." Patty thumbed the buttons to replay Action 12!'s news broadcast from the top of the hour. Aisha's statement was the normal PR crap until it came to her threat to bring in Monica.

Harri's mouth fell open when her partner told the world about Tim and Monica's affair and insinuated the new Ghost Owl was their love child. Tim was going to have a cow when he saw this.

As if on cue, Tim roared from the reception area. "HARRI!"

She buried her face in her hands. This day was getting better and better.

CHAPTER 10

Aisha kept her composure while Essie signed off, saying "We'll have more on this breaking story during our six o'clock broadcast." As soon as the director signaled they were off the air, Essie reached over and smacked Aisha's upper arm with her sheaf of notes.

"You bitch! You were holding out on me!"

Aisha raised an eyebrow. "You got the scoop of a lifetime, didn't you?"

Nella stalked over to them. "I don't appreciate being blindsided like that, Franklin."

"I know, and I apologize to both of you." Aisha sighed. "This was the only way I had to possibly get a message to Miss Purrception."

Nella crossed her arms. "Do you really think she was coerced into escaping?"

"Actually, I'm hoping she slipped up somehow, and Trubble and Black Death are tagging along because of the opportunity." Aisha grimaced. "The alternative is they forced her into helping them, which means she and Hard Knock could already be lying in a shallow grave somewhere."

Nella blanched at that thought. Even Essie looked shocked, as if she hadn't considered that particular possibility. Nella nodded slowly.

"Then we're going to need a little extra information to add to the six and eleven o'clock broadcasts," the producer said.

"I'll tell you what I can," Aisha murmured.

Once they were in Nella's office, Aisha tried not wince as Essie battered her with questions. The reporter recorded the conversation on her phone to transcribe later, but she also had a pad of paper and a pen for notes.

"So this means you know who the original Ghost Owl is?" Essie said.

"No, it doesn't," Aisha replied. "Xquic retrieved his body from the lake before anyone had the chance to unmask him."

"You're talking about a Mayan goddess, here." Nella gave Aisha an odd look.

"I know it's hard to believe, but Harri and a shit ton of FBI agents were in Westerville State Park when Xquic showed up to claim the body of the fake Captain Justice." Aisha shrugged. "Harri actually spoke with the person claiming to be Xquic and the new Ghost Owl. My partner's a pretty good judge of character. If she believes Xquic, then I'm going with Harri's statement until I see evidence otherwise."

"What did you mean by Miss Purrception's friends in Japan?" Essie asked, changing the subject.

"She assisted members of Japan's Superhero Enforcement Bureau in apprehending Professor Paranoia," Aisha said. "All I can say is a couple of our clients were involved."

"But Miss Purrfection is persona non grata in Japan," Essie protested. "Something about stealing the imperial jewels."

"She stole them to keep them out of the hands of two rival Yakuza clans who planned to use them against each other and the Japanese government," Aisha said firmly. "She returned the jewels as soon as it was safe to do so. Between that and her assistance capturing Professor Paranoia,

Japan dropped all charges against her in return for her not coming back to their country."

"Who can I talk to in the SEB?" Essie scribbled in a rapid fashion. It was a wonder her notebook didn't catch on fire from the friction.

"Captain Takashi Takeda." Aisha spelled out both names for the reporter. Rey wasn't going to like any of this, especially with the NSB showing up on their doorstep this morning. But he'd been keeping in touch with Takashi, so the SEB captain would go along with their story.

"Which American supers were involved in Professor Paranoia's capture?" Essie asked.

"I'm not at liberty to say," Aisha said firmly. "But it was with the consent and cooperation of both governments."

"Why hasn't the Department of Justice extradited Professor Paranoia?"

While Aisha personally liked the young reporter, Essie had a tenacity that would shame any pit bull. But she could be incredibly naïve sometimes.

"You'd have to ask the attorney general about that one," Aisha said with a smile. "But if I had to guess, it's probably not worth the effort because he's already serving consecutive life sentences in Japan for his crimes. Not to mention it would be difficult and dangerous to bring him here. The man has mind-control powers. With one slip-up, all his guards are dead, and he's on the loose again."

"Do you think you could line up an interview with the new Ghost Owl?" Nella's eyes shone. She was smart enough to realize the value of this story.

"I don't know." Aisha spread her fingers. "I'd need to call them and ask."

"What would it take to have him here for the six o'clock newscast?" Nella persisted.

"Can't you call him now?" Essie pleaded.

"Come on, Aisha." Nella begged, too. "All he's done so far is a few charitable appearances. Kids love him, but you know he needs the parents to love him just as much. It's how the game works."

"Nella, I don't need you lecturing me about how superhero public relations work," Aisha said, adding a hint of bitterness to her tone. "I pushed Captain Justice too hard, and I got him killed. The original Ghost Owl drowned at the bottom of Lake Del Oro because I—"

Aisha turned away. She didn't have to fake any emotions. Nightmares of Harri's still form slowly drifting toward the silt lining the basin plagued her a year after the incident. The bloody pulp Aisha had to beat Steve into to keep him from killing anybody. The raw anguish that she would never see Rey alive again.

Aisha swallowed hard. "I asked him for his help when I realized Captain Justice had been replaced by an imposter, and I got him killed for it."

"None of that was your fault." Essie laid her hand on Aisha's forearm.

"Just ask the new Ghost Owl for us," Nella murmured. "It's his call from there if he wants to be interviewed here at the studio. And Essie's right. None of what happened with Captain Justice was your fault. The supers know the risks of outing themselves."

Aisha looked at Nella. "Do they really? The new Ghost Owl and Sparx were in the process of apprehending Doctor Liquidation last month when her damn minion killed her. We assume because they have these abilities, they are morally superior. But are they really?"

Nella cocked her head. "Girl, you sound like you need a session in the confession booth at Santa Lucia." A good chunk of the Canyon Pointe population attended services at the Catholic cathedral, the oldest church in the state. Maybe, Aisha did need to confess her sins, but never to a total stranger.

Realizing how maudlin she sounded, Aisha chuckled. "You're probably right. Not to mention it'll drive my Baptist aunts crazy. I'll tender your offer to the Ghost Owl, and I'll call you if I get any answer from them." When Nella opened her mouth, Aisha held up her index finger. "But don't get your hopes up."

"Fine." Nella held up her hands in surrender. "We'll go with what little you've spoon fed us."

"Geez, Nella!" Essie gave her producer an exasperated look. "Don't piss off my source by giving her the mom guilt trip"

"Essie, I need to speak with Aisha a moment." Nella inclined her head at her office door.

The reporter leaned closer to Aisha and said sotto voce, "I hope you say yes." Essie added a wink before she rose and left Nella's office, closing the door behind her.

Aisha faced Nella and waited.

"Have you considered our offer?" Nella said tentatively. Was she that worried about Aisha not being able to compartmentalize her clients' needs from her own interests?

Aisha smiled at the producer. "So far you've only expressed interest in tendering me an offer. I'd like to hear some details before I make any decision. Plus, I do have to run any outside commitments past Harri and Susan."

Nella made a face. "Harri—"

"Isn't the sole decision maker here," Aisha said firmly.

Her statement seemed to relieve the producer. "Let me buzz Mark, and we'll head to Nolan's."

After lunch, Aisha said her goodbyes to Mark and Nella outside of the television station. Aisha marched to her minivan, climbed inside, and flipped on the A/C before she leaned back and stared at the beige headliner. The station's offer was more than generous in terms of salary. In fact, it was more than they'd paid Howard.

Which Aisha knew thanks to the staff when she still worked at Dewey and Cheatham. The partners there never really learned how to treat their staff appropriately. And the staff considered Aisha one of them, one of the few times her skin color had been a plus.

Mark, the station manager, didn't seem nonplussed about Aisha pointing out she couldn't comment on her firm's clients. The bigger question, which she didn't bring up to Mark or Nella, was what Rey would think about her taking on what was essentially a third job. It already killed her that she'd missed a couple of Mitch's milestones. The extra income meant she could cut back on legal work which was the real time consumer.

But she first had to get past Harri and Susan. They were already going to have a hissy fit when they saw the noon interview. They were going to go absolutely ballistic when they heard what Aisha planned next.

Then there was Rey and his dream of going to the Sorbonne to think of, but this might be the way to get him there faster. She just needed to convince him of that.

But first things first. She straightened in her seat and twisted her key in the ignition. Hopefully, Tim might have a lead to finding Monica before Aisha had to decide whether or not to submit to the TV interview later tonight. It was one thing to be Aisha Franklin, high-powered lawyer, in front of the cameras. It was another being Jatz'om Kuh, the new Ghost Owl.

CHAPTER 11

Harri tried to project a calm demeanor when Tim stormed into her office, but dammit, couldn't this have waited until she finished her first cup of java?

"What the hell, Harri!" The red in his face rivaled the color of his hair. "Aisha had no right to blab my personal business all over the airwaves!"

"It wasn't yours," Harri said calmly but firmly. "It was a dead vigilante's personal business."

"Quit splitting hairs!" He started pacing. "What the hell was she thinking?"

"I don't know exactly." She sighed. "Last I heard she was taping a segment for the evening broadcast. Then I wondered if this was something the two of you cooked up—"

"I didn't tell her to do this!"

Harri sighed. "But now, I think she was trying to get a message out to Monica."

"What message?" Tim threw his hands in the air while he shouted. "'I'm pretending to be your son, and I'm going to hunt you down, bitch!'"

"She specifically mentioned friends in Japan, meaning her, Rey, and

Steve," Harri pointed. "I think she's trying to get Monica to contact one of them, let them know what the hell is going on."

"Then why—" Tim clamped his jaw shut and glared at Harri's inoffensive carpet.

"—did Aisha have you start an algorithm if she was going to pull this stunt?" Harri finished for him. "She's as pissed as you are, but for different reasons."

"Why aren't you pissed, too?" Pain drew lines around Tim's eyes when he looked at her. "Out of all of us—"

"I have the hair-trigger temper?" Harri gave him a rueful smile and shook her head. "I got most of it out of my system this morning when Eddie called, ostensibly to question me about the escape. And then, I found my partners and our entire staff hiding in Aisha's office after I blew up this morning. It kind of made me realize I was acting like my dad." She snorted. "Without the benefit of illegal pharmaceuticals."

Tim pivoted and closed the door to Harri's office. He returned and pulled her into his arms. "I'm sorry for taking my anger out on you. The last thing I want is for Monica Reinhold to come between us. And I really don't like the fact we're both acting like your dad. I didn't realize how bad things were during your childhood."

"It's okay." Harri wrapped her arms around his waist and hugged him back. "Adult me understands how much emotional pain Dad was in after Mom died. And frankly, it's about time I grew up and gained control of my daddy issues."

"Well, look at Harri Winters, all grown up," Tim teased before he kissed her lightly on the lips.

She threaded her fingers through his hair and tugged his head down for a much more thorough kiss. Of course, her cell phone started ringing. She groaned and rested her forehead against Tim's chest.

"That's either Aisha or Jeremy."

"I'm not taking any bets." Tim scowled. "But if it is your law partner, I want a word with her."

Harri disengaged herself from Tim, stalked over to her desk, and picked up her cell phone. The call ID said, "Unknown Caller." Probably spam. She was about to let it go to voicemail when some instinct told her to answer it.

She thumbed the appropriate button. "Hello?"

"Listen up. I don't have a lotta time, so don't be asking me no questions," a male voice growled through the phone, but there was also the sound of trickling liquid. "Mon got your message, but they won't let her alone to talk. The idiots with us think the new Ghost Owl is the grandson of Eagle Forever. T says there was something special about the kid, but he won't tell Mon what. We'll stick with 'em as long as we can, but BD wants to get rid of us." There was a slight pause. "We're heading toward you." The line abruptly went dead.

No sense having Arthur try to trace the call. It was most likely a burner phone.

She grabbed her pen, flipped her legal pad to a clean sheet, and scribbled down the message.

"Harri?" Tim looked at her like she was crazy.

She held up index finger while she thumbed the speed dial for Aisha's phone.

"Don't start with me, Harri," her partner snapped. "I did what—"

"Stop. I wasn't calling to yell at you. Are you coming straight back to the office?"

"I was planning on it," Aisha said. "Why?"

"Your stunt worked." She grinned at Tim. "I think I just got a call from Hard Knock."

CHAPTER 12

Aisha sat on the couch in Harri's office and listened while Harri breathlessly relayed the phone call from Hard Knock to all the partners.

"You know you're killing Tim by kicking him out," Susan said. She sat beside Aisha and immediately hid her wicked grin behind her cup of tea.

"This was a message from a client, even if it was relayed by a third party," Harri said with a huff as she propped her left hip on the corner of her desk.

"Did you hear anything in the background that might indicate where Hard Knock was?" Aisha asked.

Harri crossed her arms over her chest. "Honestly, it sounded like he was taking a leak."

"Mauvaises is an eight-hour drive from here," Susan said. "They could already be in Canyon Pointe."

"That's if they take the interstate," Aisha pointed out. "We're talking four fugitives here. They'd have to get clothes and a car first. Not to mention taking the backroads to get here. The NSB finally issued a BOLO to state and local law enforcement. Monica would stay off the main roads."

"That's also assuming they come in a generally straight direction," Harri added. "They could have had help. Someone on the outside to provide civilian clothing and transportation. Not to mention, if Black Death wants to dump Monica and Hard Knock's bodies somewhere, he'd find the most isolated spot imaginable."

"That could be anywhere in a several hundred mile radius." Susan shuddered and set her mug down on the glass-topped coffee table. "Honestly, and I hate to be the one to say this, what is stopping Cade from killing them? Purrfection and Knock were only useful for getting him and Trubble out of Mauvaises."

Aisha wanted to kick herself for trying to get Monica to surrender. Tim was right not to trust her. "Oh god, she's telling them she can lead them to me and Tim."

"You and Tim?" Susan looked at her askance.

"Translation, the Ghost Owls." Harri covered her mouth for a moment before she said, "There's something that might be related to everyone's new obsession with both Ghost Owls I need to show you two upstairs."

Aisha and Susan followed Harri back to the walled-off section of her loft that formed the spare bedroom. Aisha frowned. The room itself was no longer the neat guest area it had been back at Christmas when Susan had to evacuate her parents and her sister's family down to Canyon Pointe.

Instead, the space looked like it was used by someone obsessed with tracking down a serial killer. Or maybe the lair of a serial killer herself.

Pictures of Eagle Forever, Grandma Harri, and Byron Trubble lined the top of the far wall. From there, colored string crisscrossed all over the rest of the wall, connecting photos and other documents. Gold stood for the dead superhero, blue for Grandma Harri, and red, of course, for

Trubble. Half-empty banker boxes stood along the wall to their right. From the yellowing of the cardboard surfaces, the boxes had to be twenty to thirty years old.

However, the scariest photograph was a much younger Trubble with an equally younger Grandma Harri. A woman and child stood between the two. Aisha's throat clogged. This was impossible.

"What the hell is this, Harri?" Aisha tapped the picture with her index finger. "Why on earth do you have your family photos interspersed with records regarding a dead superhero and a felon? And where did you get a picture of Trubble with your freakin' grandmother?"

"That photo was with those boxes in a storage facility Grandma Harri left to me." Harri waved at the cardboard containers neatly lined against the wall. Learning of Trubble's connection to Harri's family had to be killing her.

Susan stepped closer to the weird collage and studied it. "Oh, my god, Harri." She turned to face them. "Do you really think your grandmother was funding Corvus?"

"Not directly," Harri murmured. "She was donating to the Superhero Legal Defense Fund." She stepped closer to the wall and pointed at a listing of bank statements and tax receipts. "Eagle Forever ran it as a non-profit, but part of the money was being funneled to Ravenwood Consulting, which then sent the cash to an off-shore account."

"You're going back from before you were born." Susan tilted her head. "How are you managing to get all this documentation?"

"Some of it was in a storage locker my grandmother left to me." Harri gestured at the bankers boxes lined up against the wall. "Tim's been helping me track down the rest."

"Did he scan everything Grandma Harri left you?" Aisha asked.

Harri nodded. "I scanned most of it. He's got everything on the Owl's Nest secured server, and he probably has the info stashed offline in a couple of other places."

"Ravenwood." Susan was scanning the wall, her right index finger tracing connections. "A possible early version of Corvus?"

"That's what we think," Harri said.

The last time Aisha had seen her best friend this visibly shook up had been the day Grandma Harri died. She wrapped her arm around Harri's shoulders. "You should have told us, girl. You didn't have to take all this on by yourself."

Susan crouched to examine some more documents. She whistled before she looked up at Harri. "Let me guess. All these idiots think the original Ghost Owl is Forever Eagle's allegedly dead grandson?"

"We believe so, but Tim is definitely not related to Forever Eagle." Harri swallowed hard. "We've been trying to locate the grandson, but—"

Realization struck Aisha's brain like one of Sparx's lightning bolts. "I'm such a dumbass!"

"What?" Harri and Susan said at the same time.

Aisha blurted, "What if Miss Purrception knows who Eagle Forever's missing grandson really is, and where he's located? She's leading Trubble and Black Death to us to keep them away from the kid!"

CHAPTER 13

<hr>

Harri stared at her best friend. "What the hell are you blathering about? And Forever Eagle's grandson isn't exactly a child now."

"What she said," Susan added as she stood again.

"Screw the breastfeeding," Aisha muttered. "I need some wine and a notepad and pen to line this all out."

Susan turned to Harri. "What she said."

"It's a good thing Jeremy stocked me up when he and Leo were here for Memorial Day," Harri grumbled.

Her partners followed her back out to her kitchen. She retrieved a bottle of rosé from the refrigerator while Aisha pulled three glasses from the cupboard. Susan sat on one of the stools on the other side of the island. Harri grabbed the corkscrew from the utensil drawer and handed the bottle of wine to Aisha to pour and fished out a notepad and pen from another drawer. Aisha traded a glass of wine for the notepad and pen.

"All right, let's start with what we do know." Aisha drew a circle on the top of the page and wrote "M.P."

"Miss Purrception, AKA Missy, AKA Monica Reinhold, is a super who went to the dark side because she got knocked up by Captain Mojave, a superhero who happened to be married at the time of the affair, and lost custody of her children thanks to Trubble," Harri recited.

Susan leaned over and tapped the circle Aisha drew with Captain Mojave's initials. "He'd be about the right age to be Forever Eagle's grandson."

Aisha drew a question mark and wrote "F.E.'s grandson."

"But Mojave grew up on the reservation," Harri protested.

Aisha snorted. "And Captain Justice was an upstanding American citizen who gave his life saving the citizens of Canyon Pointe."

"All right." Harri held up her hands. "Point taken. His entire backstory could have been falsified."

"The better question is why would Monica protect Mojave," Susan mused. "He refuses to acknowledge her daughters as his even though he has to know from the way he reacted to Sourpuss."

"You mean after the way he came on to Sourpuss," Harri said bitterly.

"Hey, at least he backed off once he knew who Sourpuss's mother was," Aisha said.

Harri and Susan looked at Aisha and at the same time, said, "Ewwww!"

Aisha rolled her eyes. "Can we please move away from the attempted incest? Besides, it was never going to happen." She shrugged. "Not with Sourpuss anyway."

"Are you saying Molly would?" Harri looked at Aisha with an incredulous expression. "She's your babysitter!"

"Yell that a little louder," Aisha retorted. "I don't think she heard you in my loft, which is just across the hall."

"Come on, you two." Susan tapped her fingers on the notepad.

"We've got to figure this out if we have any hope of finding this guy and protecting him."

Aisha poised her pen, but hesitated and looked at Harri. "Are we doing the right thing? Maybe Forever Eagle's grandson is better off where he is. He's managed to stay off both the NSB and Corvus's radar for nearly sixty years. What if he's married? Hell, what if he has kids or grandkids? We could be putting them in danger."

Damn, Aisha had a good point. Harri stared at her wine glass for a long moment before she took a sip. "That leaves you, Tim, and even Mitch firmly in Trubble's crosshairs," she finally said. And she really hated the fact that Trubble was after both of her godchildren because she was damn sure the bastard hadn't given up on Grace. The slight hope of getting his own daughter back was probably the reason Black Death was still going along with Trubble's plans.

"You all have been on his hit list for a while, and I'm sure I've been added by association," Susan murmured. "However, I have to agree with Aisha. Maybe we should stop digging. At least until the fugitives have been captured."

Harri sighed. It wasn't what she wanted to hear, but she could understand Susan's concern, especially after someone broke into her family's mountain cabin and royally trashed it. "All right. I just—I was hoping you two would tell me Grandma Harri wasn't involved in this mess."

Aisha wrapped her arms around Harri and hugged her. "You know I'd be the first one trying to prove Grandma Harri's innocence. She treated me like family."

Harri patted Aisha's forearm. "You are family. So are you, Susan."

"I appreciate that." Susan smiled. "Hey, I forgot to tell you. The sheriff up in Ridge County caught the little schmucks who vandalized Mom and Dad's cabin."

"So it was just vandalism?" Aisha asked. She released Harri to take a sip from her own glass.

"Not necessarily." Susan's expression darkened. "The two twenty-somethings claim someone paid them to do it. However, they couldn't produce any names, so no plea deal. The insurance took care of the repairs, but Mom and Dad decided to sell it." She blushed, so there was obviously more to the story.

"Spit it out, girl," Aisha commanded.

Susan winced. "They had such a great time here they were wondering if they could do it again this Christmas."

Aisha looked at Harri, no doubt half-expecting her to say no, but Harri couldn't. Instead, her eyes burned with unshed tears. People wanted to be with her during the holidays. That hadn't happened in a long time.

"Actually, that would be great," she choked out. She cleared her throat before she added, "So what do we do about finding our client before Black Death puts her in a shallow grave?"

Aisha grinned. "If she's going to lead him to me on the pretense of the Ghost Owl being Forever Eagle's great-grandson, then we need to lay an Owl trap."

Harri groaned. "You've been spending too much time with my boyfriend."

However, deep down, a part of her fretted they were already too late. She didn't know if she could face Rue Liberty again if her daughter was dead.

CHAPTER 14

The elevator wheezed as it took Aisha down to the Owl's Nest. The superhero lair in the depths of the Lechuza Building was technically hers now, but as far as everyone else was concerned it was still Tim's territory, including Tim.

Which meant for her apology to be sincere, she must tread into the lion's den.

She had known during the on-air interview he'd be miffed about how she spun the Ghost Owl story. But from what Harri said as they left her loft, he'd gone totally apeshit upon seeing the clip.

Aisha had to find a way to placate him because dammit, she needed him. Needed his tech if she were going to remain the Ghost Owl. Normally, her mantra was a good offense was the best defense, but this required finesse.

And a boatload of humility.

The elevator groaned to a stop, and she pushed the gates open. The palm pad at the sealed door into the old bunker blinked green at her touch. Knowing Tim, the security system had alerted him, and he now watched her on the monitors.

She pulled the door open. The electronic hum of the secondary defensive measures faded, and she entered the hallway. Yep, he was definite-ly watching her.

And probably building a good head of steam to vent at her, too.

He had every right to be a little pissed. She could use her superspeed to reach his lab more quickly and thwart his temper's growing explosion, but that didn't seem right. So, she walked at a normal, sedate pace.

She reached the door to the main lab and raised her fist to knock when the lock clicked. Steeling herself, she shoved the door open.

Tim looked over his computer monitor, his eyes narrowed. "Aisha. Need to steal more of my life for your PR campaign?"

"Our lives," she answered. "If it saves—"

He shook his index finger at her. "Don't even think of calling Missy innocent."

"No, she's not," Aisha agreed. "But we can't have Black Death on the loose either." She stepped closer. "I am sorry I hurt your feelings. I went with a gut reaction in the middle of the interview, and I didn't take you into consideration."

Tim blew out a deep breath and looked away. "Do you have any idea how much I regret some of the shit I did after . . ." He looked at her again. This time, it wasn't fury shining from his eyes, but grief and agony. "I never thought I'd find someone again after Rebecca. I did a lot of stupid things. The thing is I thought I could talk Missy into going straight, help her get her kids back."

"Make a new family?" Aisha said.

"I was an idiot," he muttered.

Damn, Miss Purrception had really broken his heart. Aisha wanted to hug the poor guy, but it would probably be taken the wrong way. So, she chose her words carefully.

"No, you still had hope," Aisha murmured. "Despite everything that was done to you and your family, there was a piece of you that clung to hope. And even now, you don't want Rue or her granddaughters to feel the same pain you do everyday.

"I really am sorry I hurt you, but we need to keep Trubble's attention on us. Otherwise, another innocent may die."

The agony in his face was replaced by the problem solver. "What are you talking about?"

"I think Trubble believes the original Ghost Owl is Forever Eagle's grandson," she said. She relayed the conversation she had with Harri and Susan upon Harri's revelation that her grandmother may have been involved with Corvus.

Tim leaned back in his office chair and mused over her story. "That makes more sense than some of my theories. But why does he think the original Ghost Owl is still alive?"

"Come on, Tim." Aisha waved a hand. "You know the rules of the supers' game. No body, no death."

"Screw the rules." He snorted. "I'm being serious, Aisha. What's the obsession?"

Aisha shrugged. "Harri said Gil Wilcrest guessed the truth about you right before he died. Maybe Trubble has, too."

"If he had, Black Death would have already killed me," Tim said.

"Black Death was a little too obsessed over Patty and Grace last year." Aisha smirked and folded her arms over her chest. "Or Trubble didn't figure it out until he had plenty of time in prison to think."

Tim cocked his head, a perplexed look on his face. "So if Trubble thinks I'm the Ghost Owl . . ."

"Remember, the original Ghost Owl turned all that evidence over to the FBI and the Canyon Pointe D.A.'s office not too long after Forever Eagle's death." She shrugged her right shoulder. "In his mind, it would be perfectly reasonable for the grandson to seek revenge because that's what he would do."

"So what's the big deal about Forever Eagle's grandkid?" Tim asked.

"It's the same big deal about Mitch and Grace." Aisha scowled at the thought. "He tried to get control of Grace through her biological father, and he tried to extort Judge Barrowman into removing Mitch from mine and Rey's custody. Two very powerful kids with unusual abilities. My guess is there was something very special about Forever Eagle's grandson. Why else fake Lydia and the baby's deaths? I take it there was nothing in Grandma Harri's files about the kid other than the picture."

Tim shook his head. "Only his original birth certificate and the fake death certificate. And Lydia's husband allegedly committed suicide out of grief six months later."

Aisha snorted. "Suicide my ass."

"If he really thought they were gone, he might have." He stared at his computer. "Lord knows I considered it a time or two." He looked up at her again. "If I had an inkling about any of this, I would had started digging twenty-one years ago."

"You can't beat yourself up over this," Aisha said. "We've already got Harri doing it. And frankly, I'm a little pissed Grandma Harri dumped this on my dad. If Trubble had an inkling of what she had in that storage locker, my entire family would be dead, too."

"I understand your feelings," Tim said. "But I think that's why Mrs. Winters hid what was in there from your dad. He couldn't blab about what he didn't know. Plus, he considers Harri and Jeremy his kids just as much as he does you, LaShun, and Martin, so he wouldn't have said a damn word if he did look in that storage locker."

That fact that Tim held her dad in such high regard sent warm fuzzies through Aisha.

"Are we right in not trying to find Forever Eagle's grandson?" she asked.

"Maybe . . ." Tim sat up straight. "What if you ladies are on the right track? Missy knows who the grandson is, and she's taking Trubble to him for revenge."

Aisha tilted her head and regarded him. "I know Captain Mojave can be a dick, but do you really think he's capable of murder?"

"But what if it's not Captain Mojave?" Tim said. "What if it's someone else? Someone who's managed to fly under both Corvus and the NSB's radar for all this time?"

"Like Serena and her family?"

Tim nodded.

Serena Alvarez was a physician's assistant who worked at Doctor O'Brien's new clinic in the Canyon Block of the city. Her mom was a normal human, but her dad was a super who'd evaded detection because his power was registering as a normal human. He could extend his shield to other supers within a certain physical distance from him. That gift kept the NSB from taking Serena and her siblings when they were younger.

Especially since a healer like Serena was a very rare power and the government always wanted to get control of those kids.

"So either he can shield himself, or he has someone else nearby who can shield him?" Aisha mused.

"We can conjecture all we want, but—" Tim waved at his monitor. "Until we get something more than a call from Hard Knock on a burner phone, it's not going to help us."

The inner door to Arthur's work space flew open. He dashed in, and his expression brightened when he spotted Aisha. "Oh, good! You're here. We've got one!"

Adrenaline surged through Aisha. "The NSB message center?"

"The NSB message center?" Tim's puzzled switched from her to Arthur and back to her again.

Arthur nodded vigorously and handed her his phone. "This literally just came through."

Aisha stared at the screen. Bless his hacker heart! Arthur had been keeping an eye on the superhero alerts sent by the NSB's communication center. Someone had been sending out messages that were invisible even to the NSB system administrator. Like the one that had set up Rey to be captured by Professor Paranoia last year.

"I'll call Rey." Aisha handed Arthur's phone back to him. "Explain what you found to Tim while I change. And Arthur?"

"What?" He blinked owlishly at her.

"Great job." She patted his shoulder.

"Thanks." He smiled shyly.

She pulled out her phone as she left Tim's lab and headed to the room where her costumes were kept. Her husband's phone rang once. Twice.

"Is something wrong with Mitch?" Rey said. Of course, he jumped to that conclusion. The only other time she'd ever called him at work was the night she'd gone into labor. In the background, pans clattered, ceramic plates clinked, and someone with a knife was slicing vegetables from the rapid-fire chopping.

"Mitch is fine, baby." She let out a deep breath. "I need your other self. We've got a lead on Missy, but we have to beat an assassination team to her."

CHAPTER 15

Despite the prohibition her family always had about spilling dirty laundry, relief flooded Harri now that she'd told Aisha and Susan what she'd found in Grandma Harri's storage locker. Sure it was too big of a burden to put on teenage Harri, but her adult self should have been able to handle it.

Except she hadn't. At least, not very well considering how light she felt now.

She dropped into her office chair and entered her password on her laptop. The little clock on her monitor said it was after three p.m. Crap, where had the day gone? A glance at her to-do list showed nothing but Mother Defiant's intake interview crossed off. Harri sighed. She might as well start calling the superhero's references.

No sooner had Harri picked up the phone to dial the number of the first person on Mother Defiant's list when Rey swooped into her office.

Literally.

At superspeed, too.

Which sent the paperwork stack in her inbox flying all over the room.

"Sorry, Harri." Rey started picking up sheets and envelopes at superspeed, making the entire situation worse and filling the room with the smell of grilled beef and jalapenos.

"Stop!" Harri threw up her hands.

Rey halted. He was on his knees with a bunch of papers in his hands. One last sheet floated down and landed squarely on top of his head.

"Why aren't you at work?"

"Gotta a lead on Missy." He pulled the sheet off his head, carefully stood up, and handed the stack he'd retrieved to Harri. "Can you watch Mitch for a while? Molly leaves at six."

"Isn't she going with you?"

Rey shook his head. "We're not doing that to her. Can you—"

"Of course." She made a shooing motion with her free hand. "Go! Just no flying—"

"Thanks, Harri!" He dashed out her office door.

At superspeed again.

The rest of the paperwork sitting in her inbox that hadn't been disturbed by his entrance flitted through the air.

"—in the office," she finished with a sigh. So much for getting started on that to-do list. She walked around her desk and started picking up the papers on her office carpet. At a knock on the door frame, she looked up.

Patty had a sympathetic expression. "Arthur said they've got a lead on Miss Purrfection."

"Yeah, Rey asked if I could look after Mitch tonight," Harri said.

Patty chuckled. "I'm glad that blur racing past my desk really was him." She crouched next to Harri and started picking up papers. "How about we take the kids out and get some dinner since our men will be watching over the supers tonight?"

"That actually sounds like a good idea." Harri looked at her assistant. "Do you ever get jealous of the amount of time Arthur is devoting to being the new Ghost Owl's sidekick?"

"Heck no!" Patty grinned. "It's actually a blessing in disguise. I can only handle so much doting every day. Besides, it gives him purpose. That's made a huge difference in his attitude." She cocked her head and regarded Harri. "Do you get jealous of Aisha being the Ghost Owl?"

Harri stared at Patty. That wasn't the corresponding question she'd expected from her assistant. She sat back on her heels and considered Patty's query.

"I am. A little." Harri shook her head. "But it's not the superhero stuff. I expected our arrangement to be more like when we were living together in college and law school."

"When you two and Jeremy shared a crappy apartment and subsisted on noodles and popcorn?"

"I never told you that."

"Aisha did." Patty held out her hand for the papers Harri had collected. "I'll get these back in order for you."

"When did she tell you?" Harri gave her the sheaf she collected. "And why?"

"While you were luxuriating around Ultramegaperson's pool in Oakland, we had a girls' night." Patty rose to her feet. "Qiang asked Aisha if you two were trying to recreate your undergraduate life."

"You guys had a girls' night without me?" Harri stood to hide her feelings. For some reason, that hurt, which was ridiculous. She was away on business.

"Qiang is having a rough time with her parents in assisted living." Patty hugged the papers against her chest. "With Connor at camp that week and Steve in San Francisco with you, she wasn't dealing well with being alone."

"Oh."

"We could have our own girls' night," Patty offered. "I'll see if Susan wants to go with us."

"Sure." Harri nodded. "That sounds good." She gestured at the paperwork Patty held. "Was there anything in there I needed to review before the end of the day?"

"Yeah, Ultramegaperson's changes in liability insurance and the civil claim against Glass." Patty hesitated a moment. "I know it's not my business, but are you really thinking of taking on Mother Defiant as a client?"

"I don't know yet." Harri frowned. "Why?"

Patty's mouth twisted. "I didn't like the way she copped a superior attitude with me this morning when she arrived. I know it's petty, but . . ."

Anger did a slow burn through her blood. "Have you had issues with any of our other clients?"

"That's just it." Patty grimaced. "Everyone else treats me like a member of the firm even though I don't have a law degree."

Harri grinned. "Does that mean you've changed your mind about enrolling at Canyon Pointe University?" She'd brought up the offer to cover Patty's tuition more than once. The young woman had a mind for the legal profession. Her talent was wasted as a paralegal. Even more so as a receptionist/Girl Friday.

"No, and quit pushing, Harri." Patty's scowl faded. "Even Ultramegaperson is super sweet to me. They just give you crap because they enjoy getting a rise out of you."

"But Mother Defiant?" Harri prompted.

Patty walked over to Harri's office door and closed it before she walked back over to Harri. "She got pissy with me when I wouldn't let her see Susan. Then she said, I couldn't stop her if she wanted to see Susan."

The slow burn of anger inside Harri turned into an inferno. "Patty, if something like this ever happens again, you come get me."

Patty nodded. "I will. She just caught me off guard. I expect this stuff working for the city. It hasn't happened since you opened your private practice."

"Thank you for letting me know." Harri patted Patty's shoulder. "It will definitely factor into our decision."

"I'm sorry," Patty murmured.

"What? Don't be," Harri said fiercely. "There's no reason for anyone to have a diva attitude."

"Especially when they're not bringing in any money." Patty smirked.

"Hey, if Ultramegaperson treated you like that, I would have kicked their ass to the curb." Harri scowled again. "While you sort pages, I'll buzz Susan about dinner. How does Nolan's sound?"

Patty gave her a quizzical look. "You sure you want to take the kids there?"

"Yep." Harri nodded affirmatively. "And it's on me. An apology for having to put up with a twat waffle of a potential client."

"Thanks, Harri." Patty charged out of the office.

Harri reclaimed her office chair and stared at the monitor. Patty's question about Aisha hit closer to home than she realized. They were single fifteen months ago when they both quit their jobs to start this firm. Maybe she did expect Aisha to be her emotional support for the rest of their lives.

She couldn't blame Aisha though. Neither of them expected the significant changes to their lives, including marriage and babies. Aisha had everything she'd always wanted in life, and she deserved it.

Crap. Harri twirled her ponytail around her finger. Was that why she pushed Tim away every time he so much as hinted at making their relationship official? She wouldn't have an excuse to resent Aisha for abandoning her if she took the big leap into marriage again.

Disgusted with herself, she released her hair and reached for the phone receiver. She needed a night out, even if it was with her godchildren, before she drove herself crazy.

CHAPTER 16

Aisha sped through the hazy summer air, Rey tight by her side. Wind whistled slightly around the edges of her helmet. Thank goodness, their self-contained supersuits had a cooling system. Even with their speed and altitude, her visor's display said the outside temperature was in the high eighties. This heat wave had been going on for over a month now.

The coordinates on the message Arthur intercepted indicated the wetworks team dispatched to take out the fugitives would do so in Gold Reach, a small city, or large town depending on who you asked, in the northeastern corner of the state. Gold Reach sat on the edge of the Great Plains, so it contained mainly grain fields, windmill farms, and light industry.

"Why on earth would they come this way from Mauvaises Prison?" Rey murmured over the comm.

"From what Hard Knock told Harri, Black Death wants to ditch him and Miss Purrception," Aisha said. "Not too much in this section of the state, so it would be a good place to bury their bodies."

Rey snorted in her ear. "The desert would have been better. Coyotes and other scavengers would scatter the remains."

A slight chill ran through Aisha. Between Corvus and Professor Paranoia, her husband had every right to his bitterness. But Rey was beginning to sound more and more like Tim, and the similarity bothered her.

"You know I'm right," Rey added defensively.

Aisha sighed. "I'm not questioning you. None of this makes any real sense, and it won't until we find Miss Purrception."

Maybe her matter-of-fact tone had some effect. "Five minutes to interception," Rey crisply responded. He dropped in altitude. She followed suit.

Corn, clover, and wheat waved wildly in the turbulence of their passing. The air inside her suit turned a little funky as adrenaline surged through her body. Sometimes, enhanced senses could be a pain.

They passed over Pioneer Creek, the northern feeder into Lake Del Oro. The coordinates in the secret dispatch specifically pinpointed a truck stop three miles outside of the Gold Reach city limits. That was the only thing that made sense. If Monica and Hard Knock were looking to ditch Trubble and Black Death, that would be the best place for them to catch a ride away from their co-fugitives.

Aisha checked the status of the wrist launcher for her knock-out pellets and the electric stunner. She didn't know if she still had the invulnerability against Black Death that Xquic had granted her while she was pregnant with Mitch. Even Rey had agreed that they couldn't take any chances. They need to take out Trubble's personal assassin hard and fast.

Except Trubble wouldn't hesitate to take hostages, so he needed to be their second priority.

"Ready?" Rey's voice crackled in her ear.

"Ready," she confirmed.

They had little cover, so she would make the splashy distracting entrance since everyone focused on the Ghost Owl these days while Rey flew in low behind the line of big rigs at the back of the lot. It meant she would do the very thing that drove Harri so crazy when she had been the city attorney of Canyon Pointe.

Aisha dropped into a three-point landing in the middle of the truck stop's parking lot. She winced as her right fist, right knee, and left heel left deep divots in the concrete. She rose and examined the faces of the people staring at her. Families on summer vacation. Long-haul truckers. A couple of obvious sales people. No one familiar stood in the crowd. She switched on her suit's amplifier.

"Citizens, for your own safety, please return to your vehicles and leave immediately," she said. "Fugitives are known to be in this location."

If that didn't get the hit squad's attention, nothing would. The majority of the group scurried toward cars and trucks. A few paused to take pictures. Most citizens were smart enough these days to get the hell out of away when a superhero told them to do so. Too many people had learned the hard way that ignoring the warning wasn't worth their lives.

"Two men and a woman just ran into the truck stop's diner," Rey said.

Aisha turned off her suit's exterior speakers before she answered, "Anyone exiting the back doors?" Around her, cars and trucks peeled out of the parking lot and headed down the road toward the entrance ramps for the interstate. She rose a few feet into the air and pivoted to look around. More citizens exited the convenience store and the diner.

"We've got two cooks, three wait staff—" He paused for a moment, then satisfaction filled his voice. "Missy and Trubble just came out the back door."

"Crap," Aisha muttered. "How much do you want to bet the three who ran inside are our hit squad?"

"How about dinner at Nolan's?" Rey replied.

"You get Missy and Trubble out of the line of fire," Aisha said. "I'll help Black Death and Hard Knock."

"You know I hate that idea," Rey grumbled.

Aisha laughed. "I'll make it up to your manhood later tonight."

She darted for the doors into the diner. There was a loud boom right before the windows of the diner exploded outward. She automatically threw up her arms and duck to shield her face from the flying shards of glass.

Thank goodness, her helmet compensated for the sound. Otherwise, her entire head would be ringing, not just her ears. She flew through one of the destroyed windows.

To her left, a woman lay on the floor tiles, shaking like she was having a seizure. A man stood beside her, staring not at Aisha but at something else. Rather, someone else.

To her right was Black Death. The odd tickle she'd felt before said he was using his powers on her, which was a pretty good indicator of what had happened to the lady.

Aisha flew over the booth between her and Black Death, grabbed him by the collar, and slammed him into the wall. She fired a knock-out gas pellet in his face for good measure. He dropped to the ground unconscious.

She whirled around to face the other man. His fingers rested on his partner's neck. However, Aisha's suit sensors said there was no life in the still form.

The male assassin rose to his feet. With an enraged expression on his face, he reached beneath the back of his jacket and pulled out a grenade.

That explained the earlier explosion.

He yanked the pin and threw the grenade directly at Aisha's chest. She caught it and looked wildly around her. Directly outside the blown-out windows were the gas pumps, not to mention civilians were still leaving the parking lot. Other civilians were scrambling out of the diner through the kitchen or into the convenience store.

Well, the dang building was damaged already. She launched herself straight up. Once she crashed through the roof, she threw the grenade as hard as she could straight up.

And she watched in horror as a small passenger jet climbed right into her projectile's path.

CHAPTER 17

Harri set her office phone receiver in its cradle and stared at her notes. Pretty much all of Mother Defiant's references said the same thing. She was good at being a superhero, but her interpersonal skills sucked. Even Blue Racer admitted as much. Harri had to remind him of the potential conflict of interest if the firm took on his girlfriend as a client.

Harri tossed the notepad back on her desk. Aisha may have a point about Blue Racer being more of a problem since he hid his relationship with Mother Defiant from them. On the other hand, if Aisha and Susan could work their branding magic, the licensing for Mother Defiant could be quite lucrative.

Aisha and Susan had a say on whether to take on Mother Defiant, but Harri wanted to ditch her just for the way she treated Patty. An item she'd definitely bring up when the partners had a chance to talk.

Speaking of which, Harri glanced at the clock on her monitor. It had been a couple of hours since Aisha and Rey had left to intercept the Mauvaises Prison fugitives before the unknown hit squad got to them. She'd been distracting herself with reference calls and the paperwork that needed to go out before five o'clock today. But they should have arrived at Gold Reach by now.

The intercom buzzed, and Harri punched the appropriate button. "Yes?"

"Harri, Howard Dewey is on line one." Patty sounded perplexed. "He asked for Aisha first, but when I said she was out for the afternoon, he demanded you. Plus, he's refusing to tell me the reason for his call."

Harri had to agree with their assistant. Why on earth would Aisha's former employer want to talk to her? Unless this was about Mother Defiant firing his firm.

"Put him through." Harri's phone set buzzed again, and the line one button flashed.

Harri picked up the receiver and pressed the button. "This is Harri Winters."

"What do you think you're doing stealing all of my clients, you little cunt?"

It wasn't the insult that startled her so much as the vehemence with which he spat it out. She'd met the senior partner of Dewey and Cheatham a couple of times over the years at professional functions, but Dewey made it clear he regarded Harri no better than the associates he used and abused.

"You might want to rephrase your question, Mr. Dewey," Harri replied coolly.

"I know what you and Franklin are doing," he shouted. "And I will not stand by while you pick apart the firm my father built."

Harri considered her options. Part of her wanted to fling insults right back at him, but from what Aisha and his former clients had said about the bastard, he was probably recording this phone call. One wrong sentence and he'd file a complaint with the bar. One that might even stick. On the other hand, this could be a good chance to fish for some information regarding their link with Corvus. But she'd have to be very, very careful.

She tapped the button to record the conversation. Two could play that game.

"First of all, none of us here want your firm," Harri said.

"I know about Mother Defiant!"

Out of all the superheroes who'd fired Dewey and Cheatham before hiring Winters and Franklin, why did that one concern him?

Harri sighed loudly. "You're going to have to be more specific, Howard, because according to my partner Susan Kennedy, you poached Mother Defiant from her last year. And Ms. Kennedy chose not to file a grievance against your firm."

"We did no such thing," he growled. "A client has every right to choose their own representation."

"Exactly. I can't stop Mother Defiant from shopping for a new attorney any more than you can," Harri stated firmly.

"She is still under contract—"

"And she was under contract with Susan Kennedy," Harri interjected. "That didn't stop you from talking to Mother Defiant last year."

"Susan Kennedy left this firm under unpleasant circumstances—"

Enough was enough. The man couldn't keep his story straight if it were stretched out on a rack, and Harri didn't have the time or energy to listen to his tirade.

"Are you saying Mother Defiant didn't fire Dewey and Cheatham last week?" Harri said coolly. "Because I have a copy of your dismissal letter from her after I told her I couldn't talk with her unless she was unrepresented."

The spluttering sounds over the receiver sounded reminiscent of Grace blowing raspberries.

"You know you wouldn't have these kind of issues if you didn't try to take the superheroes for every last penny," Harri added, trying to sound as sympathetic as possible. "Not to mention letting Stuart Cheatham sexually harass the female attorneys, staff, and clients."

"You and Franklin are doing this to get back at me for firing her," Howard snapped at the sharp reminder of the settlement amount he had to cough up to his former receptionist Becky Roth because of Stuart.

"No, she quit your firm, and I grabbed her before anyone else did." Harri forced a loud sigh. "You should have made her a partner while you had the chance, Howard. A lot of your clients loved her, which was why they followed her to Winters and Franklin. I hope you don't make the same mistake with the next money-making female associate."

"You're going to pay for this," he hissed.

"Is that why you put the spyware on Mother Defiant's phone?" Harri leaned back in her chair and waited for the explosion.

Which never came. Interesting.

"Look, Howard, here's some friendly, non-legal advice. One senior partner to another." Harri stared at the art deco medallions on her office ceiling. "Spying on our clients isn't good business. And our clients talk to each other. By now, Mother Defiant's told who knows how many other supers about the spyware my tech guys found on her phone."

"Spyware you planted."

She could visualize the sneer on his face from the sneer in his tone.

"It was the same spyware Corvus used to try to infiltrate our firm last year." She kicked off her flats and put her feet up on her desk.

"Are you accusing Mother Defiant of being in bed with Corvus?" There was a certain glee in Howard's voice.

"Not at all." Harri smiled to herself. "I believed Mother Defiant when she proclaimed her innocence. All the FBI will have to do is check who she met with prior to her phone becoming infected. I suggested she file a report with them."

Once again, only static and the faint sound of breathing filled her ear. She waited, albeit not patiently. Maybe she should get another cup of coffee while the other attorney tried to formulate a reply.

Finally, Howard said, "You touch Captain Mojave, and I will file a grievance."

"You're in luck." Harri chuckled. "I can't because it would be a major conflict of interest."

"How so?" Real curiosity lay in his voice.

"We represent the mother of his illegitimate children."

"You're lying," he said flatly.

"By the way, tell him to keep his dick in his tights around my clients," Harri said. "Actually, that goes for you, too. If either of you propositions one of my clients again, I'll file for paternity and back child support."

Howard mumbled something Harri didn't catch before the signal died abruptly. She swung her feet off her desk, leaned forward, and re-placed her receiver in its cradle.

She had her confirmation that Dewey and Cheatham was in deep with Corvus, but the evidence she had was circumstantial. Would that be enough for Tim and Arthur to start digging into the rival law firm?

Harri hoped so because the idea of someone resurrecting the black ops organization gave her the chills. And Howard Dewey might just be stupid enough to try.

CHAPTER 18

<hr>

Aisha launched herself straight up, but she was too late. The grenade exploded as it became level with the jet's right engine. The intake sucked the shrapnel into the engine, which in turn, sounded like wolverines caught in a clothes dryer.

Black smoke billowed from the exhaust side of the engine.

"Owl, where are you?" Rey said in her ear.

"Got a secondary problem," she reported. "A grenade hit a passenger jet. They've lost an engine."

Rey muttered a few choice words in Spanish and K'iché. They were followed by a grunt.

"Falcon?"

No answer. Crap. The choice between civilians and spouse was why they rarely did the super-schtick together. Maybe she should have grabbed Cobblestone instead. However, she would have had to carry him since flight wasn't one of his talents.

Heck, then she wouldn't have had the strength left to toss the stupid grenade so far.

She crossed her fingers Rey could take care of whatever was happening on the ground. "Match transmission with the jet in front of me," she ordered the computer.

"—explosion. Right engine is gone," a male voice reported.

"Can you return to the airport, Flight 223?" a woman's voice asked. "I've cleared all the runways for an emergency landing."

"No, Tower—"

"Yes, they can," Aisha said.

"Who is this?" the woman who must be the air traffic controller demanded. "You're interfering—"

"This is Ghost Owl," Aisha said. "I'm approaching 223 from below on their right. I'll be their right engine long enough for them to land safely back at the airport."

"This is Captain Hannigan," the male voice said. "Thanks for the assist, Ghost Owl."

"You're welcome," she said automatically.

Faces peered out of the airplane's windows, a reminder of what was at stake. Aisha matched the jet's speed and dipped beneath the right wing. Tim's training lessons rang through her head. The tip wasn't strong enough to support the plane. She needed to insert herself between the damaged engine and the plane's body and exert the right amount of force to keep the plane aloft without ripping the wing off the fuselage.

She eased into position and let the wing settle along her back. The left engine's sound no longer whined like an over-revved car. "I'm into position, Captain."

"All right," Hannigan said. "Tower, our altitude is steady at ten thousand feet. I'm turning ninety degrees left. Ready, Owl?"

"Ready," she said through gritted teeth.

The jet made a swooping turn. All she had to do was keep a steady pressure along the wing and let the captain and his control of the flaps and rudder guide the craft. Through her comm system, she heard the captain and his first officer go through the landing checklist. They called out everything over the radio so she wasn't fighting against them.

After the second left turn, the captain said, "We're starting our descent, Ghost Owl. When the back wheels touch down, there will be a jolt, and your first instinct will be to grab the plane. Don't."

"You've done this before?"

"The Ms. Swift incident is part of mandatory commercial pilot training."

The Ms. Swift Incident. It was a cautionary tale for everyone from supers to the legal profession. Fifty years ago, the disaster taught the entire world that supers were just as human as everyone else. Ms. Swift had been one of the 563 who died in that accident, doing exactly what Aisha was now.

"Understood," she replied. "I'll disengage the moment you're down."

Her heart pounded as the plane slowed and descended. Her visor display showed the same number the first officer recited. The runway came closer and closer.

"Turning to the left to line up the runway," the captain reported.

The plane shifted, and Aisha moved with it. Anxiety raced up and down her body. She swallowed hard and focused on the lives she literally held on her back.

White stripes flashed beneath her. She clenched her fists to keep from doing anything stupid. The plane jolted when the rear landing gear touched down, and she dropped toward the asphalt to avoid the flaps.

The jet whizzed over her head. She held her breath as the nose gear grabbed the pavement. With the wind, aircraft noise, and smoke, she didn't notice the firetrucks pacing her until the jet came to a complete stop.

That's when the first sob forced its way from her throat. She landed and doubled over, pretending to be catching her breath, as the guilt of what she'd done consumed her.

CHAPTER 19

❖❖❖

Inside the Lechuza Building's garage, Harri carried Grace's extra car seat from her ancient Honda to Aisha's minivan while Patty and Susan carried the babies and Molly handled the diaper bags. The Garcia-Franklins owed her, not that she would have refused to babysit Mitch. But there was no freaking way Harri could get two babies and four adults into her vehicle. The cops would frown if she stuck one of them in the trunk of her sedan.

And they'd be downright pissed if any of the supers were car surfing on the Honda's roof no matter how cute they were.

Molly took the back seat with Mitch. Patty claimed the middle seat with Grace. That left Susan riding shotgun with Harri driving.

After she and Tim were attacked in Nolan's by Corvus stooges, the owners tried to offer a modest settlement to keep her from suing them. Instead, she negotiated something better—reservations for her party at any time of her choosing. The arrangement saved Nolan's owners a buttload of money and made Harri look damn good when she would wine and dine potential prospects at one of Canyon Pointe's top restaurants with a moment's notice.

"Have you heard from Aisha yet?" Susan murmured as she buckled her seatbelt.

"Not yet," Harri muttered. She inclined her head toward the back seat.

Susan got the message because she leaned back against the headrest and closed her eyes. "It feels like we packed three Mondays into a Tuesday."

Harri made the choice not to tell Molly about Aisha and Rey's mission. There was no sense in worrying the young woman. She desperately wanted a relationship with her mother. It was a pity Monica wasn't able to deliver what her daughter needed.

Molly's fraternal twin Kerry, on the other hand, would simply roll her eyes and say, "I'm not surprised." Though in some ways, she would be more disappointed than her sister.

Harri turned the key and the minivan's engine hummed to life. She backed the vehicle out of its parking spot and guided it toward the exit. So, of course, her phone started ringing.

The screen on the minivan's dashboard showed Nella's name and number. The news producer normally called Aisha, but she wouldn't be answering her cell phone. Not while she was being the Ghost Owl.

Harri tapped the hands-free control to answer the phone while she waited for a couple of cars to pass by. "Hi, Nella. This is Harri."

"Harri, do you have any comment on the Ghost Owl's rescue of a jet this afternoon?"

It took her a couple of tries to get the words out. "What are you talking about?"

"You don't know?"

"I'm taking some friends out to dinner," Harri said. "It's been a very rough day for all of us. Would you care to spell it out?"

"We had a news team up at Mesa Rojo, covering their preparations for the Captain Justice Memorial," Nella said. "They were on their way back when they got footage of the Ghost Owl saving a jet. Exactly like CJ did a year ago. Is there anything you'd like to say?"

"What are you trying to insinuate here?" Harri said incredulously.

"I want to know the truth," Nella said. "Is the new Ghost Owl Captain Justice resurrected?"

"That's utterly ridiculous!" Harri's heart tried to climb out of her throat. God, they were so stupid to think they could pull off the switch without someone becoming suspicious.

"No body, and the Owl appears about the same time Captain Justice was declared dead," Nella drawled.

"That's not true!" Molly protested.

"Shush," Patty hissed at the super.

"Who's that?" Nella said.

"Like I said, I'm taking some friends out to dinner," Harri said. "You caught us in the car."

"Papa!" Mitch hollered from the back seat.

"Ohmigod, Harri!" Molly said. "Mitch just said his first word!"

Harri felt a surge of pride. But at the same time, she was happy she hadn't pulled into traffic. Too much was coming at her at once.

"Wait a minute," Nella said. "If Mitch is with you, where's Aisha?"

"Geez, Nella, can't my partner have one romantic night with her husband?" Harri snapped. "And for your information, I've got both of my godchildren in the minivan. Want to start accusing me of running a kidnapping ring?"

Nella laughed. "If you think the crabby act is going to work with me, try again."

"Just tell me whether all the passengers and crew on that plane are okay," Harri said.

"Only bruises and cuts from the jouncing after the loss of one of the engines," Nella reported.

"Then the Law Offices of Winters and Franklin are ecstatic one of our clients assisted in saving so many lives." Harri sagged in her seat. "Is that a sufficient sound bite?"

"Is it okay if Kent leaves out the sarcasm during the late night broadcast?" the news producer chuckled.

"I'm sorry, Nella." Harri looked over at Susan, who was trying not to laugh. "It's been a hell of a day."

"I can imagine." Nella hesitated, which gave Harri ample warning but there was no way to get Molly out of the minivan before the news producer blurted, "Any news about the prison break?"

"Winters and Franklin are cooperating with the NSB," Harri stated. Damn, she did not want to discuss this in front of Molly. "We maintain it's in the best interests of Miss Purrception that she surrender to authorities, and we will do everything in our power to help her find a peaceable solution to this situation."

"You're killing me, Harri." Nella snorted. "Can't you give me a hint off the record?"

"Only thank you for broadcasting Aisha's plea for Miss Purrception to turn herself in." Harri glanced in the rearview mirror. Molly's morose expression said everything the poor girl was feeling. It reminded Harri too much of the disappointment she felt over her dad and stepmom's actions. "I wish I had something better to tell you."

"Fine. I won't interrupt Aisha and Rey's private time, but would you please call me once you hear from the Ghost Owl? Aisha was supposed to relay a request for him to be on tonight's eleven o'clock newscast."

"I'm sure she relayed your offer," Harri said. "But Susan's in the van with me and none of us have heard from the Owl yet."

"Damn, I was hoping to have him for tonight," Nella muttered. "Essie will be so disappointed."

"If I hear from him, I'll remind him of your offer," Harri promised before she and Nella exchanged goodbyes. Thankfully, both Susan and Patty kept their mouths shut about where Aisha and Rey had gone in front of Molly. Harri looked in the rearview mirror. "I'm so sorry about that, Molly. We can just pick up a carry-out order from Nolan's if you don't feel like going out."

"Nope," the younger woman said. "You promised me margaritas tonight."

"La Churro's would be a better place for drinks," Susan said.

"Except I want both a margarita and peanut butter pie tonight," Harri replied.

"So Nolan's it is." Patty clapped, which prompted Grace to gurgle and clap, too.

That seemed to cheer up everyone else in the minivan, but Harri nibbled on her lower lip. If Aisha was out in Gold Reach rescuing passenger jets, where the hell was Rey? And better yet, did they stop the assassination team dispatched to kill their wayward client and her three compatriots?

CHAPTER 20

Guilt swept through Aisha as the passengers sang the Ghost Owl's praises after they slid down the evacuation slide. It was her fault they had been in danger. More sirens wailed as additional fire trucks, ambulances, and police vehicles roared down the runway towards the damaged jet.

The smoke from the right engine permeated her supersuit and penetrated her air system despite Jeremy and Tim's design. As a result, she reeked of exhaust and jet plane fuel. She waved the passengers away from the plane and carried one elderly gentlemen, whose wheelchair was still in the cabin, over to a team of paramedics.

Some of the kids wanted autographs. She had to promise them in exchange for the children letting the paramedics look them over for injuries. However, the parents and other passengers had no problems snapping pictures of her and the damaged jet with their phones in the meantime.

A white police sergeant approached Aisha as her comm crackled to life.

"Owl, where are you?"

The sergeant opened his mouth, but Aisha held up her right index finger. "One moment, sir." She turned off her external speaker. "Baby, I'm dealing with cops at the airport. Are you all right?"

"Not when my partner takes off in the middle of apprehending wanted fugitives," he growled.

Thankfully, her visor hid her cringe from the spectators. "I'm sorry. There was a plane in trouble."

"Just come back to the truck stop. Our favorite NSB agent is already here with his team." Rey didn't sound mad. Just resigned to the inevitable.

"Give me a few minutes." She reactivated her external speaker. "Sorry about that, sergeant."

"I need to get your statement, Ghost Owl." The police sergeant seemed irritated by being told to hush.

"I was in the middle of a call with Black Falcon when you approached me," she said. "The NSB are already on site of where this all started, and I've been ordered by the agent in charge to return. It's a truck stop just a couple of miles outside of town. I'd be more than happy to take you with me so I don't have to repeat the same story multiple times."

The sergeant paled. "I'd prefer not to get carried by a superhero again, thank you." He pulled out his cell phone and jabbed at the screen. "Do you have any idea of what happened to the jet?"

Crap. The attorney part of her warred with the guilty part over what to say to the officer. Fortunately, the attorney part won.

"I'm not sure, but it might be debris from our attempt to apprehend the four fugitives from Mauvaises Prison," she replied.

"The BOLO we got about Miss Purrception, Hard Knock, and Black Death?"

"Yes, sir."

The sergeant gestured in the general direction of the interstate. "Then go! But I still need that statement. I'll follow up with your agent."

Aisha didn't need to be told twice. She launched herself skyward.

From the air, the damage to the truck stop didn't look quite as bad. Except for the huge hole she'd left on the roof. She landed lightly beside Rey and Agent Nesmith.

"Nice of you to join us, Ghost Owl." Nesmith's lips twitched like he wanted to smirk, but he managed not to, which probably saved his life.

"Next time, I'll let the jet crash," she snapped. "Then I'll be here faster."

Nesmith and Rey looked at each other, then back at her. "What jet?" they said in unison.

A junior agent raced up to Nesmith. "Sir, we just got a report that the Ghost Owl—" The kid's double-take when he recognized her superhero togs would have been hysterical in other circumstances. "Should we still go to the Gold Reach Regional Airport, sir?"

"Naw," Nesmith drawled. He cocked his head. "You didn't leave there without talking to the commander on the scene, did you?"

Aisha shrugged. "I don't know if he was the commander, but I told the sergeant, who started to speak with me once the passengers and crew were safely out of the plane, that you and Black Falcon needed me back here."

"That explains why you stink of smoke and fuel." Nesmith turned back to the younger NSB agent. "Eastwood, tell the commander on the scene I'll send him a full report since his situation is connected to ours."

"Yes, sir." The kid trotted off to join the rest of the agents taking pictures of the truck stop and samples. Four agents strode out of the diner, carrying a body bag.

"Please tell me no one else died in this mess besides the assassin who Black Death killed," Aisha murmured.

"Let's start at the beginning, you two." Nesmith gestured emphatically at the truck stop. "How'd you know about our escapees being here?"

"We had an anonymous tip," Rey growled.

Nesmith gave them both a skeptical look. "Does this have anything to do with Owl's threat delivered by your attorney?"

"Sort of," Aisha replied. "Hard Knock got away from Trubble and Black Death long enough to call Harri Winters. She contacted us. We arrived here just as a wetworks squad made their attempt on the fugitives."

"I had Trubble and Miss Purrception dead to rights when they came out the back door of the diner," Falcon said.

Aisha could feel her husband glare at her through his visor. It was a good thing neither of them had laser vision.

"Hard Knock caught me from behind," Rey continued. "He must have been hiding in one of the rigs parked along the back of the lot. I tried to subdue him, but I had to let him, Miss Purrception, and Trubble go." He rubbed the back of his neck.

"Why?" Nesmith's tone wasn't accusatory, more like encouraging Rey to continue.

"The two male assassins came out the back with a mother and her son as hostages," Rey said.

"Those are the two guys you had hog-tied along with Black Death?"

Rey nodded.

Aisha wanted to sink into the ground in relief. The fugitive she worried about the most was in custody.

Nesmith eyed her. "Owl?"

Aisha recited her side of the story including how she accidentally tossed the damn grenade in the path of the passenger jet. She waited for the NSB agent to harangue her about putting civilians in danger.

"Oh, come on, Owl." Nesmith groaned. "Do I have to give you the lecture about not ditching your partner? Again?"

"This was different. Lives were at stake," Aisha bit out.

"Did you say anything to the cop back at the airport?" He scribbled in his notebook.

"Only that it might have been debris while we were trying to arrest the Mauvaises Prison fugitives," she said.

"Good." Nesmith snapped his notebook closed. "That's the story we'll stick with."

"What about the assassins?" Rey asked.

"The dead woman has already been identified as a former CIA operative who disappeared on a mission five years ago." Nesmith rubbed his lower jaw. "I only know that because I met her personally at a joint training exercise ten years ago. The other two we need to identify." He smiled. "Though if you identify them before I call you. I'd appreciate a heads-up."

"And you're really going to call us?" Suspicion ran through Aisha.

"Yeah, I will." Nesmith regarded her. "You don't trust me, and after what happened to Captain Justice and your predecessor, I don't blame you. I know I'm going to have to earn it. And Owl?"

"Yes?"

"Sometimes, Murphy's Law kicks in, and there's nothing you can do except clean up the mess," he said. "I know you're kicking yourself behind that face shield so stop it."

He gestured to the spectators watching and taking pictures beyond the area cordoned off by the NSB. "Why don't you two go do the hero press-the-flesh and sign some autographs? It'll keep the civilians out of my people's hair long enough to finish our investigation." He started to turn back to the diner.

"Wait," Rey said. When Nesmith faced him again, Rey continued, "How did you know the fugitives were here?"

"Your attorney wasn't the only one who got an anonymous call." Nesmith grinned. "Black Death called us."

<h1 style="text-align:center">CHAPTER 21</h1>

After drinks, dinner, and a lot of peanut butter pie, Harri drove back to the Lechuza Building. Susan offered her guest bedroom to let Molly sleep off her three margaritas. Thankfully, Molly was tipsy enough to agree that it was better she not ride her motorcycle tonight.

Harri texted Tim before her little party left the restaurant. He could certainly come out to the garage to carry his and Arthur's dinners into the building since she had her hands full with Mitch. She'd also ordered to-go meals for Aisha and Rey.

Tim was waiting in the garage when she guided the minivan into its parking space. He grabbed the bags out of the cargo area while Harri, Patty, and Susan took their respective sleepy charges.

"Anything from our wayward fliers?" Harri asked softly as they trooped into the building.

"Their ETA is fifteen minutes," he said as they followed everyone into the building. "Anything else we need to bring in from the minivan?"

"No, we got it all," Harri replied.

Tim looked up at the security camera aimed at the garage door and nodded. The security panel beeped, and the magnetic locks hummed.

Everyone was quiet on the elevator ride to the fourth floor. Not because both children had fallen to sleep in their carriers, but because it had been one freaking long, emotional day.

When the elevator ground to a stop, Susan took the bag with Arthur's dinner in one hand and guided Molly with the other. "I'll be up once I get my houseguest settled for the night."

"Good night," Harri whispered to Patty and Grace. Patty waggled three free fingers before they followed Susan and Molly down the hallway. Grace merely burbled in her sleep.

Tim managed to wrestle the elevator gates closed, and the car continued its upward climb. Instead of their own loft, Harri headed for Aisha's place and punched in the key code. By the time she changed Mitch's diaper and had him settled in his crib, she heard the door of the loft roll open and more than one voice in the main living area.

Footsteps shuffled behind her. Harri turned around to find Aisha entering Mitch's room.

"Thanks for watching him tonight," she murmured.

"Hey, I'll always be there for my godson," Harri whispered back.

Aisha reached into the crib and stroked Mitch's curls. Something more than capturing the escapees and averting a plane crash had happened. Harri could sense the tension coming off her partner.

"Come on." She wrapped her arm around Aisha's waist. "Let's get you some food, and you can tell me all about it."

***

The law partners, Tim, and Rey gathered around the island in Aisha's kitchen. Rey and Tim went across the hall and grabbed a couple of stools from Harri's loft so there were seats for everyone.

Over prime rib, loaded baked potatoes, and green beans for those who hadn't eaten supper yet, Aisha and Rey relayed everything that happened during the course of their little trip to Gold Reach. Aisha's guilt was obvious when she spoke about the incident with the commuter jet.

Susan reached across the island countertop and squeezed Aisha's hand. "Girl, every superhero has that one stupid thing that happens to them."

"Yeah," Harri said. "Look at what happened to Skyball." Everyone laughed as quietly as they could with Mitch asleep close by.

Aisha eyed the baby monitor as she wiped tears from her cheeks. "I suppose I should be grateful the engine didn't burn off my costume."

"I'd enjoy it," Rey said with a lascivious waggle of his eyebrows.

"Really?" Aisha replied dryly. "You'd want to public to get the full monty of your wife and the mother of your child."

"Okay, maybe not that." Rey grinned sheepishly.

"My question is why is Nesmith so damned determined to win our trust." Tim angrily stabbed the last couple of beans in his take-out carton and shoved them in his mouth.

"I thought you ran a background check on him," Harri said.

Tim chewed and swallowed. "I did, both the legal and the illegal variety."

Susan groaned and put her face in her hands. "How many times do I have to tell you and Arthur not to mention this shit in front of me?"

"Quit being a baby, Susan," Harri growled before she looked at Tim again. "I take it you found nothing?"

Tim grinned. "Depends on what you mean by nothing. His record wasn't so clean to arouse suspicion that it's fake. A few speeding tickets, a reprimand for roughing up The Minute Man after the asshole tried to blow up a busload of nuns and children, but the worst thing he was busted for was a panty raid in college."

"A panty raid?" Harri rolled her eyes. "Was he trying to relive his dad's dreams?"

Tim shrugged. "It was the Eighties. Kids did stupid shit."

Aisha chuckled. "And there wasn't a proliferation of cell phones and web cameras at the time to capture that stupid shit. Now where's the pie?"

"Aw, crap, I forgot to tell you Nella called me on our way to dinner." Harri paused in reaching for the silverware drawer. "Something about the Ghost Owl doing an interview on the late news."

Aisha muttered an obscenity as she leaned over to check the clock on the microwave. "I need to call her and tell her the Ghost Owl is not going to make it tonight."

"No," Susan said sharply. "Let me or Harri do it. The story Harri gave Nella was that you were having a date night with Rey since we had Mitch with us." Susan glared at Aisha. "Which, by the way, I should have been apprised of as the Ghost Owl attorney of record."

"Been a little busy today with the Mauvaises escape," Aisha snapped back and slid off her stool.

Harri pitched her voice an octave lower so they didn't wake Mitch. "Quit bickering and serve the damn pie while I call Nella. What does she want from the Ghost Owl anyway?"

"A formal statement about what the supers are doing to capture the Mauvaises fugitives," Aisha replied as she opened the refrigerator to retrieve the pies.

"What about the early morning newscast?" Harri pulled her phone from her pocket.

"Bitch, I am not getting up at four in the morning." Aisha glared at her over the refrigerator door.

"Tell Nella the Ghost Owl will be there at nine a.m.," Susan said while she retrieved the silverware and plates. "As long as Aisha sticks to the official story, it will be some good publicity after the airplane mishap."

Aisha flashed the bird at Susan, which showed just how tired she was. Or that Susan had really become part of their weird little family.

Harri stepped away and tapped the redial for Nella's phone. She half-expected it to roll over to voice-mail, but Nella answered breathlessly, "What's the word, Harri?"

"Aisha did get ahold of the Ghost Owl and relayed your request, but—"

"The plane rescue happened, and he's not coming." The disappointment rolled through Nella's voice.

"What about nine a.m. tomorrow morning?" Harri suggested. "That way you can advertise the exclusive interview in tonight's broadcast, and it will give you and Essie a chance to e-mail Susan the questions to review with the Ghost Owl."

"Sounds good, Harri," Nella said. "Thanks for returning my call."

"De nada," Harri said. She ended the call, stuffed her phone back in her pants pocket, and sauntered back to the island.

"Well?" Aisha and Susan said at the same time.

"You're on for tomorrow's Morning Show at nine a.m." She climbed on her stool with a sigh and dug her fork into her second piece of Nolan's pie for the evening. "We need to talk about our potential new client—"

"Before we start on a new topic, there's something I need to tell you about since it affects my family and the partnership," Aisha said in rush. She wobbled on her stool.

Rey grabbed her around her waist. "Deep breaths, baby. Nothing is worth me pulling you off the ceiling."

Damn, this was big if Aisha was so nervous about telling them her news, she was losing control of her powers.

Aisha took a couple of deep breaths and released them. "Action 12! wants to hire me as their new on-air legal analyst. I told Nella and Mark I would have to discuss this with you all."

"You as in Aisha Franklin, kickass attorney, right?" Harri said.

This time, Aisha flipped Harri the bird.

"You don't have to discuss this with me," Tim quipped. "I'm not a partner, and I'm not married to you."

Aisha's laugh was half-hearted. "We both know Harri would tell you anyway, so you might as well stay."

"That's fabulous!" At everyone's dirty looks, Susan winced. "Sorry, didn't mean to be so loud." She jumped off her stool, ran around the is-land, and hugged Aisha. "They couldn't pick a better lawyer. Plus, this is free publicity for the firm."

The truth hit Harri about Howard Dewey's weird phone call. She couldn't stop the giggle that burbled out of her mouth. It quickly turned into a full-throated guffaw. She leapt off her own stool, raced to the couch, and buried her face in a throw pillow. The lack of oxygen got her laughter under control.

"What the hell, Harri?" Aisha looked at her crossly. "I didn't expect you to be happy about this, but laughing at me?"

"Don't." Harri waved her hands wildly and swallowed the humor threatening to erupt again. "Don't. I'm happy for you. I really am. But now, I know what Howard Dewey's nasty phone call late this afternoon was really about."

"What?" Aisha said.

Susan made a face. "You didn't say a word at dinner about him."

Harri filled her partners in on her earlier conversation with their former boss. But it was Tim and Rey who became enraged on Harri's behalf.

"Do I need to make a visit to Mr. Dewey?" Rey growled.

Aisha frowned at her husband. "Baby, you are not ruining Black Falcon's reputation. We've worked too hard—"

"You think he should get away with this?" Rey stared at her with an incredulous expression.

"We're winning by treating our clients right." Aisha waved at Harri. "He threw out some impotent threats because even if he makes up some complaint, the truth will come out. And we won't stoop to his level."

"Plus, I got a circumstantial affirmation Dewey either knows about or is part of Corvus," Harri said.

"Or losing Mother Defiant was the last straw for him," Tim said.

"What if he planned to push her into sleeping with him?" Aisha said. When everyone looked at her, she shrugged. "Getting physical with Essie Morales was part of the reason his contract wasn't renewed with the station."

Susan snorted. "That's Stuart's department."

Aisha smirked. "Cheatham hasn't touched anyone since—"

"We sued his ass for sexual harassment?" Harri offered.

Aisha cleared her throat. "That and he got a midnight visit from the Ghost Owl."

"I didn't—" Tim's genius brain took a couple of seconds to put two and two together. "Oh."

Harri stared at her best friend. She wasn't sure what to say, but Aisha playing the Ghost of Christmas Present was one of the better uses of superpowers Harri had heard.

Surprisingly, it was Susan who exploded.

"What the hell were you thinking, Aisha?" Susan waved her fork and the bite of pie on it went flying across the kitchen and splattered across a couple of cabinets. "You could have been arrested for breaking and entering!"

"Shush," Rey hissed, but it was too late. A matching wail came from the baby monitor and Mitch's bedroom. "Nobody better touch my pie." He rose from his stool and strode toward the hallway leading to the bedrooms.

"Dammit, I hate it when clients do stupid shit, especially when they know better," Susan muttered.

"Do you always trash your client's kitchens in retaliation?" Aisha snapped.

Susan slid off her stool and stalked toward the sink. She yanked off a couple sheets of paper towels, dampened them, and started wiping up the peanut butter pie smeared on the two cupboard doors.

"Just promise me you won't do it again," Susan pleaded while she dropped the paper towels into the trash.

"I won't as long as Stuart doesn't do anything else stupid." Aisha leaned her elbows on the island countertop and turned to Harri. "I expected you to do the shouting, not Susan."

Harri shrugged. "I agree with you. If you scared the little shit straight, it was worth the risk." She looked at Tim. "You want the extra curricular project of digging into the Dewey and Cheatham partners, or should I give it to Arthur?"

"I'll do it. Arthur has his hands full with the Ghost Owl's special project." Tim shot a peculiar look at Aisha.

Harri groaned. "Are you trying to piss me off tonight?"

"Not on purpose." Aisha folded her hands and rested her chin on them. "Arthur has been hacking into the NSB message center database. I wasn't satisfied with the results of their so-called investigation into the summons Rey received the morning Professor Paranoia kidnapped him."

"And?" Harri prompted.

"Someone's using the NSB system to set up superheroes and send assignments to hit squads like the one we encountered in Gold Reach today. They're using invisible characters so not even the system admin can see or access these records."

Shock and worry raced through Harri, and she sagged on her stool. "So Corvus is still active despite our best efforts."

"We think it may be someone else," Tim said. "Whoever it was wanted both Trubble and Black Death dead. Missy and Hard Knock were to be . . . collateral damage."

"Whatever happened to the days when my biggest problem with a client was paparazzi shots at a nude beach?" Susan sat on her stool with the second pie and served herself another slice.

"Pass the pie," Harri muttered. "I need to think about this."

Now, who the hell besides Miss Purrception wanted Trubble dead bad enough they would risk attracting attention with a bunch of possible civilian deaths?

CHAPTER 22

An hour later, Aisha switched off the lights and exited the bathroom. Rey marked the page of his book and set it on his nightstand. The shiny platform bedframe had been Tim and Miguel's wedding present. It was constructed of titanium so it could withstand day-to-day normal usage by two supers. And it was definitely easier to get in and out of while pregnant. Otherwise, Aisha would have had to hover to get out of her previous Japanese-style, very low platform bed. But then, she believed she would never conceive again when she bought the latter furniture. She crawled onto the mattress and cuddled in the crook of Rey's shoulder.

"Are you still mad at me about this afternoon?"

He sighed and squeezed her against his body. "No. Nesmith is right. I did my fair share of accidental damage the first few years I had my powers. But—" Rey hesitated. "—would you be pissed at me if I said we shouldn't team up any more?"

"So you *are* mad at me?"

"Not at you," he murmured. "I'm partly angry with myself for risking both of our son's parents today."

She couldn't blame him. The same thought ran through her head when she saw the families that had been on the passenger jet.

Rey continued before she could say anything. "However, I'm more ticked off about Missy doing something stupid after she swore up and down she wanted a relationship with Molly and Kerry again."

"I'm not happy with her on that note either." Aisha needed to let him know the rest of the story. "Harri believes Trubble thinks I'm Forever Eagle's great-grandson."

"What?" Rey burst out laughing.

"Keep it down," Aisha murmured. "I don't want to wake Mitch again."

"That's ridiculous," Rey said more quietly. "Where did she get that idea?"

Aisha told him about the mysterious contents of Grandma Harri's storage locker and how Harri was obsessed with the information she found.

"That doesn't sound like the woman you, Harri, and Jeremy have described," Rey said.

"Tell me about it." Aisha sighed. "I think Susan and I have convinced her to stop searching for Forever Eagle's real grandson for now. If the kid is still alive, he's stayed off Corvus's and the NSB's radar for all these years."

"Well, he wouldn't exactly be a child now, so he could be married and have kids. Maybe even grandkids," Rey said. "If we did find him, it could put his whole family in danger. Maybe it would be better if none of us looked for him." He paused a moment, then softly chuckled. "Captain Mojave would be about the right age. It might be worth it to sic Harri on him."

Aisha giggled. "True. But if we went after every man of that age in Canyon Pointe, we'd have to start with Miguel. Mayor Benevides. Heck, even Judge Inunza."

Rey snickered. "From what Arthur said, I can't envision the judge as the type to hide from anything."

"Also, true." Aisha sighed again. "For all we know, we're chasing a ghost."

"Mmmm," Rey agreed. He was silent for so long she thought he'd fallen asleep until he said, "Baby, why do you really want to take the job at the TV station? I thought we had a plan for Paris."

"Honestly, I'm looking at it as a way to get you there faster," she said.

"If I'm working at the restaurant and the construction firm, and you're practicing law and doing the legal analyst gig, where does that leave Mitch?" he asked.

"I've been thinking about that, too." She rolled onto her side and propped her head on her fist. "It's time I push Harri and Susan into hiring an associate. We haven't even started looking because we're all so damn busy. It's only going to get worse. Not to mention Steve has another two years of school before he can be licensed."

Rey rolled his eyes. "You know Harri's trying to push Patty into getting her law degree."

It warmed Aisha's heart that for once, his gesture of irritation wasn't aimed at his twin brother. "I don't blame Patty for not wanting to." Aisha smiled. "She wants to enjoy time with Grace."

"Which brings us back to our own son." Rey rolled on his side to face her. "Have you even told Harri and Susan about our plan?"

"Not yet." Aisha chewed on her bottom lip. "Harri—"

"Will bulldoze you into not going in a heartbeat if you let her," Rey finished.

"Oh, like you can stand up to her." Aisha couldn't help the derisive tone in her voice.

"Hey, I kicked her out of the delivery room when she got on your nerves," Rey shot back. "You couldn't even do that."

"I was worried enough about accidentally breaking your fingers," Aisha protested. "Her hands wouldn't have stood a chance."

Rey raised his right eyebrow. "You need to tell her soon, and not the day we're headed to the airport."

"I will. I swear." She kissed him. "Now, turn out the light. We both need to get some sleep before Mitch wakes up."

Rey rolled on his back and reached over to turn off his reading lamp. Aisha curled against his side once again. Within a few minutes, her husband's breathing deepened and slowed.

However, her mind roiled with everything that had happened that day. And part of her couldn't help but wonder whether Forever Eagle's grandson might really be the key to whoever was behind the wetworks team sent after Trubble and the rest of the Mauvaises fugitives.

The only good thing about the whole day was Black Death was off the streets again.

CHAPTER 23

The next morning, Harri stood with her cup of coffee in the spare bedroom and stared at the wall of pictures and string. Not even a hot shower and the cinnamon concoction in her mug could drive away the chill from the nightmare that had awakened her. What was it about Forever Eagle's grandson that made him so important to both Trubble and Grandma Harri?

If Grandma Harri double-crossed Trubble to get Lydia and her son away from Corvus, it would explain some of the retired general's animosity towards Harri herself. Or was Grandma Harri's financial support of Corvus, the real reason Seismic Shift and the other Corvus cronies kept trying to kill her last year? Did they believe Harri herself know more than she did about Corvus's activities, especially if Grandma Harri was funding them?

"I thought Aisha and Susan convinced you to let this go for now."

Harri turned to find Tim leaning against the doorjamb and watching her with his own mug of coffee in his hand. "I told them I wouldn't pursue it to get them off my back." She turned back to her wall of connections. "If Trubble thinks the original Ghost Owl was Forever Eagle's grandson, the reason everyone is so interested in finding the Owl's body has something to do with his powers."

"Except I don't have any," Tim pointed out.

"True." She turned to face him again. "But as you said, if Trubble knew the truth, he would have had you killed a long time ago. What about the urban legend version of Ghost Owl? Supposedly, he could dematerialize into mist. Teleport. Read minds."

"Are you saying my misdirections went a little too well?" Tim sipped his coffee.

Harri looked at her charts again and tapped her lips with her index finger. "That's what I'm thinking." She turned back to Tim and cocked her head. "The most consistent stories are that no supervillains' powers worked against the Ghost Owl and no superhero was able to track him, much less capture him."

Tim laughed. "That's because all of them are too prissy to use the sewer system."

"What if Forever Eagle's grandson could go further and actually prevent a super from using their powers?" Harri watched him to see how he'd react to the insane theory that woke her at five this morning.

"Disruption of abilities?" Tim's eyebrows formed a "V" above his dark blue eyes. "There's never been a known super who could do that."

"Yeah, the only thing that comes closest I'm aware of is Mr. Alvarez's ability to cloak powers from detection," Harri commented.

"If they could replicate the ability and it was permanent . . ."

Tim's dawning horror matched the nightmare that had awoken Harri. Her godchildren alone. Powerless. At the mercy of someone like Trubble or Professor Paranoia.

"Holy shit," he muttered. "Then what the hell is Missy really planning?"

"I don't know." Harri shook her head. "But I'm pretty sure all of our guesses so far about her motivations are wrong. I think I need to have a personal heart-to-heart with Carol this morning. The last thing I want is the Inunzas in the crosshairs of whoever is behind this."

⁓

Harri's little white lie about forgetting to put a hair appointment at Jeremy's salon on her calendar worked a little too well with her partners and staff. Aisha sent her Ghost Owl costume with Harri to see if he could get the jet fuels stains out of it. Otherwise, Aisha needed him to manufacture a replacement. Harri would have to drop it off once she was done with her errand.

She pulled into a parking space at the Inunza and Cervantes offices. It was a medium-sized, one-story building that Carol and her partner had bought for a song at a bankruptcy sale. They used half of the building for their practice and rented the other half to an insurance agency.

Carol's assistant Ngoc frowned when Harri strode in the law firm's reception area. "Ms. Winters? I don't have you listed as a scheduled appointment."

"This is an unofficial visit." Harri smiled. "I was on this side of town for another matter and I popped in to see if Carol was available for lunch."

"One moment." Ngoc held up her index finger before she lifted the receiver and pressed a button on her phone set. Her fingernails were even more wildly decorated than Aisha's used to be before she delivered a baby. Long nails and diaper changes did not go well together.

"Harri Winters is here to see you," Ngoc said crisply. "Lunch." Another pause. "Yes, ma'am." She looked up at Harri as she hung up the receiver. "She said to go back to her office."

"Thanks, Ngoc." Harri crossed to the entrance to the back offices, and when the electronic lock buzzed, she pulled the door open.

Inunza and Cervantes' security wasn't as heavy as Winters and Franklin, but then they mainly dealt with regular folks and non-supers accused of crimes. Most people didn't realize Ngoc was also part of the law firm's security. She had the ability to create force fields, but when Harri had asked her why she didn't go the superhero route, Ngoc laughed and said, "Because I know the idiots in this country who fetishize the supers don't want to see a short, overweight, middle-aged Vietnamese-American woman in tights. It ruins their precious fantasies."

Harri strode down the hall to Carol's corner office and knocked on the partially open door before she peered around the edge. Carol was pacing in front of her desk while on the phone. She gestured for Harri to enter as she said, "It was a minor fender bender in the parking lot of a grocery store, Cal. Going inside the store to call for the police because her cell phone was dead is not a hit-and-run. My client never left the premises."

Carol held out the receiver and flipped the bird at it before returning the device to her ear. "You're right. We will see what a jury says about it." She waved the receiver a couple of times as if she wanted to throw it.

Instead, she took a deep breath and placed the receiver gently in its cradle before she smiled at Harri. "This is a pleasant surprise."

"A lot better than dealing with the D.A.?" Harri nodded at the phone.

"After getting the position thanks to his predecessor's scandal, I get why Calvin Johnson needs to show he's tough on crime, but sometimes, he just pushes things too far." Carol rolled her eyes.

"Should I ask?" Harri grinned.

"You heard most of it." Carol threw her hands up. "My client wasn't even at fault for the accident. The owner of the other vehicle is throwing a hissy fit, claiming my client left the scene of the accident."

"Wait a minute." Harri frowned. "If the owner of the car that hit your client wasn't driving—"

"Her boyfriend was driving because she was too drunk." Carol laughed. "It gets better. He's in jail because he had outstanding warrants."

Harri shook her head. "Why didn't one of the baby prosecutors let this one go before it got to Cal?"

"Beats me." Carol shrugged. "Isn't he your partner's ex-husband?"

"Yep."

"Damn, I can see why Aisha left the smug little son-of-a-bitch," Carol muttered.

Harri didn't correct her about who left who. Aisha was happy now after all the bullshit Cal put her through. However, Harri still had fantasies about burying Cal in a shallow grave after he cheated on Aisha and then blamed her for his transgressions.

"Ngoc told you why I'm here. Are you free?"

Carol circled her desk and pulled out her purse. "Yep, and you're buying after the bitchy morning I've had."

Harri tried not to wince. She was about to make Carol's day worse, and she didn't think picking up the lunch tab would cover it.

CHAPTER 24

Aisha felt a little more relaxed now her interview as Ghost Owl was out of the way. It went smoothly, but she had a weird feeling Essie had a celebrity crush on the Ghost Owl. Well, she set up her superhero persona so the public could apply their own fantasies to who they thought was the Ghost Owl, so she kind of deserved the uncomfortable feeling.

Now that she was back in the office, she munched on the taco salad Patty had picked up for her from Marta's while she read the proposal for a new line of cosmetics that a top company wanted Sparx to be the spokeswoman for. They had already signed Nix for their line aimed at teen and twenty-something consumers, but the president of the company wanted someone else for older customers.

According to him, Sparx had the highest Q-score out of any cis-het female superhero, and the initial offer reflected her popularity. Aisha wasn't sure how Qiang would take the news. The brittle woman had softened a bit since she started dating Aisha's brother-in-law Steve, but Qiang hated this kind of endorsement.

Hell, she hated all endorsements, but with two elderly parents to support and a special needs son, she needed all the cash she could lay her hands on.

Aisha scribbled some ideas on her notepad. She reached for her fork when an alert from her NSB app sounded on her phone. She thumbed the controls to see it.

Ghost Owl – Miss Purrception and Hard Knock sighted at Northside Mall food court. Apprehend. Deadly force authorized.

What the hell? "Deadly force authorized"? In the middle of a busy civilian shopping center? Aisha waited, but there was no additional message, and no mention of Trubble.

So much for lunch. Aisha closed the take-out container, grabbed her keys, and stalked over to the break room to stick her lunch in the fridge. The other half of her taco salad would be a soggy mess when she returned, but she was the one who signed up for the superhero life.

However, their assistant's desk was empty when she walked into the reception area.

"Patty?"

"In here!" came her voice from the conference room.

Aisha walked in to find Patty and Susan eating their lunch with an LSAT book on the table between them.

"Don't tell Harri." Patty's glare was mitigated by the food in her mouth as she spoke.

"That's your business." Aisha held up her hands. "I was just letting you know I'll be out of the office for a few hours. NSB call."

The door to the basement slammed open and Arthur raced toward her. "Don't go! It's a set-up!"

***

The staff gathered downstairs in the computer lab. Arthur sat at his desk and pulled up the NSB message center database while everyone else looked over his shoulders. He tapped a button to show the text Aisha had just received.

"See it's the same login with the invisible characters." Arthur tapped another key, but the characters on the screen looked like weird emoticons to Aisha. "The login in shows gibberish because they're non-ASCII characters."

Patty patted him on the shoulders. "Sweetheart, not everyone speaks computer like you and Tim do."

Arthur swiveled in his chair to look up at the three women. "Whoever wrote the code for the database created a backdoor that recognizes non-alphanumeric characters. If the sysadmin runs any report on users, the code only pulls those users that have alphanumeric characters in their user names. In other words, if it starts with a letter or a number, he can see it."

"But if it starts with the airplane icon, he can't," Aisha murmured.

Arthur nodded.

Aisha crossed her arms over her chest. "So, it's a test to see if the Ghost Owl has broken their code."

"That would be my guess," Tim said. "If you take someone with you, they'll know. If you don't show up, they'll know."

Aisha smirked. "What if I call Agent Nesmith who has repeatedly lectured the Ghost Owl about not taking on the bad guys by herself, and ask him who's supposed to accompany the Ghost Owl to the scene?"

Tim grinned back. "That would work."

Aisha pulled her phone from her slacks pocket, blocked her phone's ID, and tapped the speed dial for the local NSB office.

"National Superhero Bureau. How may I direct your call?" an efficient-sounding woman said.

"Ghost Owl for Special Agent Nesmith," Aisha said. Tim had set up the software in her phone to make her voice match the sound alteration in her helmet.

After a moment, the line clicked and a male voice she recognized said, "Nesmith here."

"I heard you when you advised me not going into a scene alone and not ditching my partner," she said. "Who's accompanying me to Northside Mall to apprehend Miss Purrception and Hard Knock?"

"What are you talking about?" In the background, someone snapped their fingers, and voices murmured about tracing a call and the NSB message center.

"I'm talking about the text I just received with their location and that the use of lethal force was authorized."

"Owl, no such message was sent by the NSB," Nesmith snapped. "And you know damn well terminations are against NSB policy."

"Then you'd better bring the cavalry because someone's planning a bloodbath." Aisha abruptly cut off the call. Who in the city besides her and Rey could handle Hard Knock? Captain Mojave was out on the off chance he was Forever Eagle's missing grandson. That left one other heavy hitter.

She scrolled through her contacts and pressed a number.

"Hello?" The gravelly bass was reassuring.

"Cobblestone, it's Owl. You feel up to pounding some bad guys?"

"When and where?"

"Northside Mall. You at home?" she asked.

"Just watching my soaps," he said.

"I'll pick you up in five and fill you in on the particulars."

They both signed off the call.

"I'll grab an extra comm for Cobblestone and meet you at the exit," Tim said before he headed for his workshop.

"Be careful." Patty grabbed Aisha in a tight hug. "I don't want Mitch and Molly both losing their parents today."

"I'll do my best," Aisha said. When Patty released her, she added, "Don't tell Molly where I've gone."

"We won't," Susan said. "But the kid's smart. She's going to figure it out when she sees the helicopter footage on the news."

Aisha charged for the changing room. She had on her spare Ghost Owl uniform, except for the helmet, when Tim entered the room with the extra comm.

"Break a leg," he said as he handed the device to her.

She tucked the comm into the left breast pocket on her jacket. When she reached for her helmet, some odd emotion flickered across Tim's face.

"Do you miss it that much?" she asked.

"Sometimes." A rueful smile crossed his features. "I think I got addicted to the adrenaline rush."

"I can understand that." Aisha smiled back before she slipped on her helmet and locked it into place.

Her boots left the floor, and she shot toward the exit into the old subway station. Yep, she could totally understand Tim's addiction because she was already deep in its grip.

CHAPTER 25

Harri had to give props to the bistro Carol selected for lunch. The food was excellent. And since they came ahead of the rush, they were seated in a private alcove.

"So what did you really want to talk to me about, Harri?" Carol forked a bit of her chicken pecan salad into her mouth.

Harri slathered butter on her parmesan roll and tried to figure out a way to say her suspicions gently enough not to panic the other attorney, but also say them sincerely enough Carol would take her seriously.

"I thought it would be best to talk about Miss Purrfection face to face." Harri laid down her knife and her roll on her plate. "There's no easy way to say this, and I know how crazy it sounds. Trubble and a lot of other people believe the original Ghost Owl is Forever Eagle's grandson."

Carol stopped chewing and stared at Harri. She finally swallowed her bite of salad and said, "You're right. You do sound crazy."

"I'm not done." Harri pushed her plate to the side and rested her elbows on the table. "I have reason to believe Monica also knows the identity of the grandson, she knows it's not the original Ghost Owl, and she's leading Trubble on a wild goose chase. I just can't figure out where or why. I was hoping she might have dropped a clue with you, even by accident of what she's up to, because my partners and I think she's in way over her head."

Carol sighed and placed her fork in her bowl. "Harri, the deaths of Forever Eagle's family are a documented fact. That's the whole reason he came out of the superhero closet. He didn't have anyone to protect."

"Let's just say I have proof that Lydia Baxter-Murray and her infant son were alive after that accident." Harri reached for her water and sipped some to moisten her dry mouth. "I just don't know why hers and her baby's deaths were faked. How could she do that to her father? Or was Forever Eagle in on it, and he was that good of an actor?"

Carol delicately dabbed at her mouth with her napkin before she looked at Harri again. "That is a serious buttload of crap to unpack over lunch."

"Believe me, I know," Harri said. "Did Monica ever talk to you about Forever Eagle or anyone else? Maybe someone related to Corvus?"

"The only people she spoke about with me was her kids, her mom, and of course, how much she blamed Trubble for screwing up her life. Do you really suspect Forever Eagle's family is still alive?" Carol asked.

"Probably just the grandson." Harri waved her right hand. "Plus whatever kids and grandkids he may have had."

Carol looked around them to make sure they were still alone. "Do you know the grandson's identity?"

Harri shrugged. "All we have are suspicions. My money's on Captain Mojave, but as Aisha pointed out to me and Susan this morning, a lot of men fit the age including our building manager and your husband."

Carol laughed, but it sounded forced. "Pablo as the secret grandson of Forever Eagle? He'll love hearing that." She turned serious again. "How do you know the original Ghost Owl wasn't Forever Eagle's grandson?"

"Let's just say the new Ghost Owl is a client, and their genetic pattern definitely won't match if Linwood Baxter's body is exhumed." Harri grinned.

Carol shook her head. "I can't imagine living down that kind of legacy, but I give the new kid props for trying."

"Me, too," Harri answered. "But back to Miss Purrception?"

Carol propped her elbows on the table and rested her chin on top of her folded hands. "Monica didn't say a damn thing to me about the Ghost Owl or Forever Eagle. Whatever she's up to, she's playing it close to the vest."

"Damn," Harri grumbled. "I was hoping she'd let something, anything, slip to you."

"Why do you think she'd talk to me before you?" Carol's neatly plucked eyebrows scrunched together. "You're the one who she turned to when she decided to surrender."

"And obviously, she lied her ass off to me." Harri leaned back in her chair. "We have an additional concern. My head of security is worried the people after the Ghost Owl may come after you and your family because your association with our firm."

"I appreciate Tim's concern." Carol smiled. "But they have no reason to fear us, do they?"

"Once upon a time, I would have said the same thing about me and Seismic Shift," Harri stated.

"I promise I'll run everything you said past Pablo. If we need to upgrade our home system, we will." Carol glared out the window a moment before she turned back to Harri. "You know we won't put Paul's life at risk."

"I know you wouldn't," Harri said. "That's the reason Tim and I wanted to make sure you and Pablo understood the potential danger."

Carol relaxed her arms and reached for her purse. "Well, I don't know about you, but I have a ton of work back at my office."

"You're not the only one." Harri pushed back her chair and stood. "I'm glad you were free for lunch."

Carol chuckled. "I'm glad you paid."

Harri laughed as well. "It's nice to talk to an adult for once during my day."

Heat smacked Harri in the face as they exited the bistro. "These hundred degree days are getting ridiculous. We need to recruit a super with ice powers to come to Canyon Pointe."

"That would be nice, but we've got to have some humidity for them to work with," Carol said.

The heat was even worse inside Harri's car, and it had been sitting in the shadiest spot on the street for less than an hour. She started her ancient sedan, but the A/C couldn't deliver more than a breeze slightly less than body temperature through the vents.

"I really need to get this fixed," Harri muttered.

"You really need to get a new car." Carol laughed. "You're not working for the city any more."

"Yeah, but this is the first car I bought with my own money." Harri checked her mirrors before she pulled out into traffic. "It's practically a family antique now." They were halfway back to Carol's office when the supervillain alert sounded over Harri's equally antique radio.

"This is a warning of the Supervillain Alert System. The National Superhero Bureau warns all citizens of Canyon Pointe and surrounding areas to stay away from Northside Mall. It is currently being evacuated due to suspected supervillain activity. The Ghost Owl and Cobblestone were seen heading toward the mall. Again, the National Superhero Bureau warns all citizens of Canyon Pointe and surrounding—"

Harri turned off the damn radio. What the hell was going on? But she didn't dare call the office with Carol in her car.

"Looks like I've got even more work waiting for me," Harri quipped. "If you don't mind, I'll drop you in front of your door—"

"I'm going to have to insist on you coming into my office with me, Harri."

"Are you kidding? I've got two clients probably about to demolish one of the profitable malls left in Canyon Pointe."

"Exactly. The Ghost Owl is your client, so he'll bring Miss Purrception and Trubble to me instead of turning them over to the NSB."

"Are you insane—" Harri glanced at Carol.

Who held a gun in her right hand, aimed at Harri.

"Never mind," she grumbled. "Now I know who provided the clothes and transportation for the Mauvaises escapees."

CHAPTER 26

Aisha's comm crackled in her ear as she flew toward Northside Mall while carrying Cobblestone. Even with her superstrength, he was pretty damn heavy.

"Owl, our mysterious friends just dispatched another hit team, and the NSB has issued an alert," Arthur reported.

Cobblestone laughed. She felt his ribs vibrate more than she heard the sound of his voice. "You do know how to attract the trouble, kid."

"It's my milkshake, man. It brings all the supervillains to my city."

Her comment only made Cobblestone laugh even harder.

"Did you guys get a hold of Paloma before the alert went out?" Aisha asked. Marta's eldest daughter managed a lingerie store at Northside. She'd helped Aisha and Rey when Corvus was trying to kill them last year. She owed the young woman her life.

"Yes," Tim said. "She evacuated her own shoppers and employees before she warned her fellow managers at her end of the mall."

"Dammit, tell her to get her ass out of there," Aisha snapped. "I am not telling her mama Paloma got herself killed by being stupid."

"Copy that," Tim answered.

In the distance, sirens wailed, but if she and Cobblestone waited for reinforcements, the three fugitives might slip away again. Aisha dove for the section of the mall that held the food court. She set Cobblestone on his feet before she landed lightly beside him.

"Nice job." Cobblestone examined the pavement beneath his bare feet. "No divots in the concrete. Harri would be proud."

"You haven't had to listen to her whine about them for fifteen years straight."

Aisha opened the door and strode into the mall's food court. It was empty except for Miss Purrception, Hard Knock, and Trubble. They sat at a table with wrappers and empty cups on it. Well, almost empty. Hard Knock slurped his smoothie from one of the kiosks.

Like they were any other people grabbing lunch while they shopped.

"I told you Owl would come," Miss Purrception purred.

"You did send an engraved invitation, Missy," Aisha replied.

"But he brought company." Trubble scowled at the two superheroes.

"And that's why I insisted on bringing Hard Knock with me," Miss Purrception answered. "Knock, you want to escort Mr. Cobblestone outside while the general and I speak with the Ghost Owl."

Hard Knock slurped the last of his smoothie. "Sure thing, Missy. It's been a while since I've taken out the trash."

"Cobblestone?" Aisha said.

"I got this one," he answered. "You take care of—"

The rest of his sentence was lost in the horrendous noise when Hard Knock bull rushed Cobblestone through the steel and glass doors and out into the parking lot.

"Enough is enough, Monica," Aisha growled. "The NSB are on their way here."

"Except there's someone you might want to talk to before you do anything stupid, Owl." Miss Purrception's smile was pure evil as she held up a phone. "Like maybe one of our attorneys." She pressed the speaker function on the phone.

"Talk," someone ordered.

The next voice was definitely Harri's. "Owl, Carol Inunza has gone wackadoodle. She and Miss Purrception are working togeth—" She cried out in pain, and every fiber of Aisha's being wanted to smack the smug grin off Monica's face.

"I've got a gun on your attorney, Ghost Owl," Carol said. "You come quietly with Miss Purrception and Trubble, and I'll let her go. It's that simple. You're the one we want. Not Harri."

Aisha watched both Monica and Trubble for some indication of their plan. How the hell did Harri go from a hair appointment at Jeremy's salon to Carol holding a gun on her?

Unless Carol had been blackmailed. The technique was one of Trubble's signature moves.

"Fine, you win," Aisha said.

Outside the broken and smashed doors, it sounded like a demolition derby as Cobblestone battled Hard Knock in the parking lot.

"That's assuming your vehicle hasn't been smashed," she added.

Chapter 27

◆━━━◆◆◆━━━◆

Inside Carol's corner office, Harri stared at the deranged attorney and the steel barrel she pointed at Harri's face. She massaged the section of scalp where Carol had yanked her hair to interrupt her from talking to Aisha.

Carol hadn't bothered to search Harri's purse. She'd already tossed Harri's phone out of the car window on the way back to the Inunza and Cervantes offices. If Harri could grab the modified taser Tim had given her, this hostage situation could be over in a matter of minutes.

"Explain this to me because I don't get it." Harri continued to rub the burning spot on the crown of her head. "Did our sisterhood of chocolate mean nothing at Jeremy's Christmas party?

"This isn't personal, Harri." Carol shook her head, her expression actually sad. "But I have to protect my husband and my son."

"Dammit, Carol. If Trubble is blackmailing you—"

"You don't get it." Carol waved the gun. "The Ghost Owl should have killed Byron Trubble when he had the chance. The man's not only dangerous. He's cruel and inhuman."

Realization slowly dawned on Harri. "Oh, my god. You and Miss Purrception have been planning to kill Trubble all along. You both just used me?"

"I was wondering where your brilliant legal mind went," Carol sneered.

"I still don't get why Trubble's murder is worth both yours and Pablo's careers," Harri said. "And what about Paul? Do you think seeing his mother in prison for murder won't scar the kid for life?"

"It's better than him ending up in a government lab and getting dissected!" The gun in Carol's hand shook along with the rest of her body. Uncertainty glimmered in her dark eyes.

"Carol, if Paul's a super, I can help," Harri said softly. "Not all of them suit up. Some even become doctors and lawyers because they'd rather assist people in other ways than with their powers."

"Harri, for your own sake, you need to shut up." Carol swallowed hard. "I'll let you go once Miss Purrception arrives with Trubble and the Ghost Owl."

"You can't," Harri said sadly. "We both know you can't. Once you kill Trubble, you and Monica will have to kill me and Owl because we're witnesses."

The gun shook even more violently in Carol's grip.

"Carol, it's not too late to reconsider what you're planning to do," Harri pleaded. "Let me call in some of my clients. They take Monica and Trubble back to prison. I won't press charges. You don't want murder on your conscience."

The intercom buzzed. "They're here, Ms. Inunza," Ngoc reported.

Harri's heart tried to leap out of her chest. For all of Aisha's abilities, this was going to go south in a hurry. Ngoc only had to hold the Owl in one of her force fields long enough for Carol or Monica to shoot Trubble. Then they'd kill Aisha, probably by Ngoc smothering her with the said force field. And then, Harri would die after watching her best friend slowly asphyxiate.

The Ghost Owl walked into the office first, followed by Trubble then Miss Purrception and Ngoc.

"You okay, Harri?" It was still a little weird hearing the suit's vocal modulator make Aisha's throaty voice sound almost masculine.

"Other than Carol ripping out the expensive highlights you made me get, I'm just peachy," Harri grumbled.

Aisha tried to take a step towards Harri, but she moved like she was stuck in quicksand. "What the—? Ngoc, let me go!"

"Sorry, dude. No can do."

"I've been waiting for this moment for a long time." Trubble rubbed his hands together gleefully.

"Have you been watching too many superhero movies, Byron?" Harri snapped.

"I just want to know who's been a pain in my backside all these years before I dissect the little bastard." He reached for the Ghost Owl's helmet.

"Are you sure you want to do that in here?" Miss Purrception asked.

"He's probably got some kind of comm inside the damn helmet," Trubble snapped.

Miss Purrception snorted. "You're worse than a kid peeking at his Christmas presents."

"I don't want him calling for help." Trubble unlatched the helmet from the rest of the Owl's costume and lifted it straight up. He stepped back, the shocked look on his face would have been enjoyable if Harri wasn't facing hers and Aisha's imminent deaths.

Aisha smirked at Trubble before she said, "Boo!"

<h1 style="text-align:center">CHAPTER 28</h1>

Despite the situation, Aisha enjoyed the shocked look on Trubble's face. Carol and Ngoc's were almost as comical.

"This is a con job!" Trubble roared. He whirled to face Monica. "You tricked me!" He took one step and froze in place.

"You got them both, Ngoc?" Monica asked.

"Yep," the receptionist answered. "No problem."

Monica strode over to Trubble and delivered a right cross that would have left any super reeling. "I didn't trick you, you piece of shit. You convinced yourself the new Ghost Owl was a descendent of Forever Eagle's."

"Slut!" Trubble spat out the word along with his blood.

"Carol, keep your weapon on Harri while I tie up the asshat." Monica nodded at Aisha's helmet. "And we need to get rid of that. Their staff will be listening in on comm system inside."

"How'd you hack the NSB messenger system?" Aisha asked. "You've been driving Tim and Arthur crazy trying to figure out how you did it. And while we're at it, why'd you tell me to kill you? You had to have known I wouldn't obey such an order."

Monica hesitated for a split second before she smiled. "Wow! I'm shocked Red and Professor Venom haven't figured it out."

Even Trubble looked surprised by Aisha's question.

Harri met Aisha's gaze. "So we've got another player in the game. Is that who you're really working for, Monica?"

"I pay my debts." The supervillain shrugged as she pulled rope from the bag she had retrieved from the trunk. "This person asked a small favor, and I plan to deliver on their wish list."

"What?" Carol looked flabbergasted. "You said we were going to kill the bastard!"

"Someone else wants asshole here alive." Monica shook her head sadly. "And let's face it, Carol. You are not a killer."

"That wasn't our agreement!" Carol shrieked.

Monica paused in tying up Trubble and gave the attorney a disgusted look. "Then shoot Harri and get it over with."

Aisha tensed. If she could overload Ngoc while she tried to hold Aisha and Trubble, she might have a chance to get to Harri and get her clear before the shooting started.

"That wasn't the plan either," Carol said through gritted teeth.

"Why the hell do you even want me dead?" Trubble asked. "The slut I understand, but why you?"

Carol clenched her jaw.

Aisha looked at Harri who gave a slight nod of her head. So her partner suspected or knew why Carol had gone off the deep end.

"I-I—" Carol started to lower her weapon when suddenly Aisha was free. A soft whizzing sound was followed by a *crack*.

Ngoc wore a surprised look on her face, but it was the bullet hole in the middle of her forehead that turned Aisha's stomach. Harri was smart enough to dive for the carpet.

Monica delivered a roundhouse kick Aisha managed to block. She shot a knock-out pellet at the supervillain. Monica shifted just enough to the left that the pellet missed her and hit Carol square in the chest. The attorney's eyes rolled into the back of her head. Her gun slipped from her grip and landed on her desk before she dropped to the floor.

Bullets started flying everywhere. All of them came from outside the office.

Aisha snatched her helmet and dove to the carpet to cover Harri with her body.

Monica slung the bound Trubble over her shoulder and ran out of the office.

"Go get her!" Harri yelled over the gunfire blazing away outside of the building.

"Are you all right?" Aisha pushed up on her hands, scanning Harri for blood.

"I'm fine! Get that bitch!" she roared.

Aisha slipped her helmet back on and latched it before she rolled to her feet and raced after Miss Purrception. She wouldn't have gone out the front door. Monica was practically obsessed with back doors.

The sound of a pneumatic door closing came from Aisha's right. Her prey moved away from the sounds of people yelling and shooting at the front of the building. Aisha raced down the hallway and hit the door. It flew off its hinges.

And standing twenty feet in front of her was a masked man in black with a long black tube on his right shoulder. He fired.

The object was smaller than a rocket. It bounced off her jacket and into her gloved hands.

"Crap. Not another grenade."

Her visor shut down from the blinding white light as the explosion propelled her backwards.

Chapter 29

The explosion rattled Carol's office hard enough folders fell off her desk and state code manuals were knocked from her bookcases. The gunfire outside stopped. Harri waited for nearly a minute to make sure none of the chaos started up again before she climbed to her knees.

A dark figure stepped into Carol's office. Harri lunged forward and grabbed her former co-counsel's gun from where it lay on the desk.

"Harri, it's me." Rey pushed his visor up so she could see his face.

"Crap." She sagged back on her heels and set the gun back on Carol's desk. "That's a good way to get yourself shot."

Rey slid his visor back in place and crossed over to Carol's limp form. He pulled off a glove and checked her pulse. "I don't see any injuries." He pulled a set of cuffs from his utility belt and secured Carol's wrists.

"Owl hit her with a knock-out pellet," Harri said. "By the way, I'm fine. Thanks for asking."

"You were talking so I didn't expect otherwise." He rose and helped her to her feet. "Where's our fugitives?"

"Miss Purrception took off with a hogtied Trubble," Harri said. The entire situation made her want to hit something. Or someone. Preferably, Monica's perfect nose. "Owl went after them. What about the staff?"

"Nix is helping me clear the building," Rey reported. "So far, it's just been superficial cuts from flying glass. Nesmith, I've got two more civilians back in the southwest corner office. One of them is the attorney who took Harri Winters hostage."

Rey cocked his head as he listened to the NSB agent. "She's here. Just a moment." Rey fished in his left breast pocket and produced a comm unit. "Nesmith wants to talk to you."

She inserted the device in her left ear. "I'm here, Agent."

"Miss Purrfection got away with the assholes shooting at my people," he growled. "I've got a report Trubble looked to be her prisoner."

"It's true," Harri said. "She triple-crossed everyone. Hopefully, Ghost Owl nabs her before she gets far."

"What are you talking about?" He sounded perplexed. "I thought Owl was with you."

"No, Owl went after Miss Purrfection."

"No one saw Owl leave the building," Nesmith stated.

Harri looked up at Rey. "Oh, my god. The explosion."

He tore off at superspeed. The wind of his passing flipped her hair all over the place. She took one step to chase him and remembered the damn gun. She picked it up, emptied out the bullets, and set the weapon behind a plant that managed to stay on top of one of Carol's bookshelves. Not sure what to do with the bullets, she shoved them in her left pants pocket before she ran after Rey.

The dust in the air pointed his direction. She turned the corner and skidded to a stop. A good chunk of the wall and ceiling were gone. Well, not gone. Late afternoon sunlight shone on a pile of debris at the end of the corridor with dust motes dancing in the rays. One gray boot stuck out at the base of the rubble.

Harri's heart stopped.

Rey dug through the plaster and brick at superspeed, shouting "Owl!" The additional dust he raised forced Harri to pull up the lapel of her blouse and cover her nose so she could breathe. Once he got everything off Aisha, Harri stepped closer.

Cracks covered the Ghost Owl's visor and helmet. Burn marks and shrapnel marred the front and arms of Aisha's jacket. Her gloves were black and smoldering.

Harri knelt beside her best friend. Chunks of debris dug into her knees as she carefully tugged off Aisha's right glove. Luckily, she only had minor burns. Harri's fingers sought the pulse point at the base of Aisha's wrist.

"I guess I should be glad you're only holding my hand, instead of kissing me and claiming its CPR," a weak familiar voice said.

"Screw you, bitch." Harri swiped at the tear creating a trickle of mud on her cheek.

"The NSB is listening on this frequency," Rey reminded them.

"Miss Purrception?" Aisha asked.

"Got away," Harri said.

"Cobblestone?"

"He says you owe him a case of beer for using him to distract and arrest Hard Knock." Rey chuckled.

Harri patted the back of Aisha's hand. "Let's get you to a doctor."

"No." Aisha yanked her hand back and struggled to sit up. "We need to get the judge and his son to safety."

"Yeah," Harri said softly. "Yeah, we do."

And she hated the fact that she'd be destroying the career of one of the best criminal judges their state had ever seen in the process.

CHAPTER 30

Aisha and Harri sat in Aisha's minivan a couple of houses down from the Inunzas' home. It was still too freaking hot outside to not have the van's A/C running. Paul was already home from his lifeguard job, and the judge should be pulling into the driveway any minute. The news of Carol's arrest would hit the wires soon. Aisha just hoped Nesmith could delay it long enough for them to get Carol's family to safety.

"I can't believe you got Nesmith to let us tell Judge Inunza what is going on," Aisha murmured.

"There's more to it than that," Harri said. "I think something you said as a joke yesterday when I told you about Grandma Harri's storage unit may be closer to the truth than either of us realized."

Aisha frowned. "What joke? I do not remember doing much joking yesterday."

"Well, you did just have part of a building fall on your head," Harri quipped.

"I can still kick your ass to the moon," Aisha snapped. She didn't want to admit to anyone, not even Rey, she had a horrendous headache. All he would do would be to fuss over her more than he already did at Carol's office. If that didn't telegraph that Black Falcon and the Ghost Owl were in a relationship, nothing else would.

But she probably did have a concussion. She'd definitely call Selena when she got home.

"You still haven't told me why it's so important that we provide the judge's protection," Aisha protested.

"Because—" Harri started, but a silver sedan pulled into the Inunzas' driveway. "He's here. Let's go." She already had her door open.

Aisha pressed the button to kill her minivan's engine, opened the driver side door, and climbed out. She caught up with Harri as she strode toward their target.

"Judge Inunza!" Harri waved.

The judge's surprised expression turned to a wry smile. "To what do I owe this visit from Canyon Pointe's top superhero attorneys?"

"You'd better not let anyone from Dewey and Cheatham hear you say that," Aisha warned.

"We're sorry to bother you at home, Judge, but we really need to talk to you privately," Harri said.

"This sounds serious." The judge's gaze flicked between the two of them, attempting to suss out what was going on.

"It's about Paul's safety," Harri added.

"You know we wouldn't be here if it weren't important," Aisha said. "Trust us. You don't want us to discuss this on the street."

"All right." He grabbed his briefcase out of the back seat and locked his sedan. "Come on in, ladies."

They entered the foyer just in time for Paul to race out of the living room. "Dad! Mom's been arrested!" He resembled his dad so much, he could have been a clone, from his blue-black hair to his broad chest and muscular legs. His bare feet slid to a stop on the polished hard wood. "Sorry, I didn't realize—"

Judge Inunza exhaled heavily. "I take it that's what you two ladies came here to tell me."

"Yes," Aisha said.

"There's more," Harri said.

"This wasn't a simple misdemeanor, was it?" he said.

"No, sir," the women said in unison.

"Paul, go up to your room."

"But, Dad—"

Aisha gestured at the teenager. "With all due respect, Judge, Paul is eighteen, and this affects him, too."

"All right." The judge waved at the entrance to the living room. "Let's sit down and tell me what you have to say."

Once everyone was seated, Aisha glanced at Harri. "Carol kidnapped Harri at gunpoint this afternoon."

"Mom would never—" Paul protested, but his father raised a hand and the teenager closed his mouth.

"I'm not pressing charges," Harri stated. "She used me to lure the Ghost Owl into a trap. The real problem is she helped Miss Purrception, Hard Knock, Black Death, and Byron Trubble escape from Mauvaises Prison two nights ago."

"I've got a friend who specializes in super criminal defense," Aisha said. "He and I will help in any way we can, including representing Carol."

The judge frowned at her. "Why would you do that?"

"Because I'm a mother, too." Lightning flashed Aisha's brain as she realized what Harri had already figured out. "And because she was trying to protect you and Paul by saying the original Ghost Owl was Forever Eagle's allegedly dead grandson."

The judge stared at the carpet for a long time before he looked over at his son.

"You know the truth, don't you, Your Honor?" Harri murmured.

"Yes. I guess it had to come out some time." Inunza sighed wearily. "You ladies are right. It's me."

CHAPTER 31

One of Byron Trubble's captors struck him across the face again. The coppery taste of fresh blood filled his mouth, and one of his teeth was loose. His wrists and ankles ached where the ropes bit into his swelling skin. Not taking his heart medication was exerting its own toll on his body as much if not more than the beating. It was . . . interesting being on the receiving end of an interrogation.

The three people on the room all wore ski masks, but the bright lights they shone in his eyes prevented him from distinguishing any memorable features. With no windows in the black-painted room, there was no way to tell how much time had passed. And the question they asked him was always the same.

"Where are the children you stole?"

"I don't know what you're talking about." Or that's what Trubble tried to say. It sounded rather garbled to his ears, too, with the swelling in his mouth and jaw.

A piercing whistle sounded in the room. The captor who was currently beating on him stepped back and laughed.

"You had your chance, old man. You should have told me what the boss wanted to know."

The sound of a door opening came from behind him, but Trubble couldn't turn his head far enough to see what was back there. It simply hurt too much.

"Out," a female said. An older woman from the sound of her voice.

The three captors trooped out of the room from the change in pitch of their bootsteps. An elderly woman tottered into view. Her back was now humped with age, and she walked with a cane. Decades ago, she'd had ramrod straight posture, a glorious blond mane, and a rack that would make even the saints themselves weep.

She pulled the stool closer and sat down. The overhead lights glinted off her now silver hair. Even now, she was the one person he feared besides the senior Harriet Winters, and Winters was long dead.

Rue Liberty smiled sweetly at him. "Oh, Byron. I hear you've been less than cooperative with my young associates."

She held up her right hand. Her torch manifested in a blaze of light. "Now, I want the full list of children with superpowers you've stolen over the years. Each time I ask, and you don't tell me, I will burn off a bit of your flesh, starting with your tiny little dick."

⁂

Oh, boy! How are Harri and Aisha going to protect the Inunza family from the people hunting for them? And what the heck is Rue Liberty up to? Turn the page for their next adventure, *Hero Amicus Curiae*!

Hero Amicus Curiae

Aisha Franklin sat next to Carol Inunza at the defendant's table in Canyon Pointe's district federal courtroom. Her law partner Harri Winters had refused to press charges against Carol for kidnapping her. However, their fellow attorney couldn't escape the charges for aiding and abetting the prison break of four inmates from Mauvaises, the federal super security prison specifically for those people classified as supervillains.

"I still don't understand why you're doing this," Carol murmured. She wore an orange jumpsuit and had what Harri referred to as "jail stink". Aisha had never noticed the odor before she had powers. Harri claimed Aisha's smoking had deadened her nose to the funk. But with the super senses her mother-in-law gifted her, the odor was a million times worse than a skunk.

"Because your husband did me a solid when former Canyon Pointe D.A. Michaels had Harri arrested on trumped up charges," Aisha said.

"Pablo wouldn't do a 'favor' for anyone with a case in his court," Carol whispered. "He followed the law. Always."

"Right now, I'm thinking you should have followed in his footsteps," Aisha hissed back.

"Hi, Aisha!"

She looked up at Jim Duncan's cheery greeting. The federal prosecutor was still as good-looking as he had been in law school. He was a sweetheart in life, but in the courtroom, he was a freaking bull shark. She was kind of glad she was only handling the arraignment.

"Hey, Jim."

"Can we talk for a moment?" He inclined his head toward the empty jury box.

"Of course." She turned to Carol. "I'll be right back." She stood and strode over to Jim.

He lowered his voice. "My boss is refusing to offer a plea deal."

"My client cooperated and told everything she knows about Miss Purrception and Trubble," Aisha whispered.

"She's also a member of the bar in a city that had a huge scandal in its D.A.'s office last year." Jim crossed his arms. "If it helps, I believe Carol thought she was protecting her husband and son. But I can't get a plea deal to fly. Not right now."

"Did you argue the money coming out of the taxpayers' pockets by taking this to trial? Not to mention burying an upstanding judge as collateral damage?"

"Girlfriend, give me a little credit." Jim made a "give me a break" face at her.

"What about bail?"

Jim shook his head.

Aisha nodded. "Okay. Thanks for trying." She returned to her seat.

"What did he say?" Carol whispered.

"No leeway," Aisha murmured. "His boss thinks your case is a slam dunk."

"Damn." Carol stared at her shackled wrists. "I'm so screwed if I go to prison."

"Don't give up just yet," Aisha said. "Let's give the judge a chance."

Carol snorted softly. "I've been in front of Judge Castillo before as an attorney. He likes throwing books at people."

Aisha kept her mouth shut. She didn't want to give Carol false hope, but maybe she could get the judge to recuse himself.

"All rise," the U.S. marshal acting as bailiff called out. "The United States District Court, District of Mojave, is now in session. The Honorable Judge Francis Castillo presiding."

The judge strode into the courtroom. He was medium height with salt and pepper hair and beard.

The bang of the public doors of the courtroom crashing open made everyone look. Masked people in black rushed inside, armed to the teeth. They fired into the air. Shrieks filled the room. The bailiff didn't even have a chance to draw his weapon before he went down in a spray of blood.

Instinctually, Aisha pulled Carol off her chair and down to the carpeted floor before she covered her client's body with her own.

"Get on the floor!" one of the assailants yelled. Everybody, including Judge Castillo, hit the carpet.

Someone poked something metal in Aisha's back. She tensed, waiting for the bullet that would tell the whole world she was a super.

"Are you Franklin?" a gruff voice said.

"Yes." Aisha raised her hands. "I'll cooperate. Please don't hurt anyone else."

"Get up," he ordered.

She slowly and carefully got to her feet.

He slammed an item on the defendant's table. "Call the Ghost Owl. We want him in return for the hostages."

Aisha stared at the phone. Well, crap. Maybe hiding her superhero identity's gender wasn't such a smart move after all.

❖❖

Acknowledgements

As always, much gratitude goes to Elaina Lee, Jaye Manus, and Darling Husband for getting me through another book. And many thanks to my friends Angie, Becky, Jo, Roshonda, and Shelley for keeping me sane as we continue to shelter in place through the 2020 global pandemic.

Suzan Harden transitioned from writing information technology manuals for companies and legal articles for a law enforcement magazine to her first love, fantasy and science fiction in all their forms. She's the author of the Bloodlines, the 888-555-HERO, and the Justice series.